SOUL
CLAP
HANDS
AND
SING

SOUL
CLAP
HANDS
AND
SING

Paule Marshall

HOWARD
UNIVERSITY
PRESS
1988

Printed in the United States of America

10 9 8 7 6 5 4 3

Library of Congress Cataloging-in-Publication Data

Marshall, Paule, 1929 –
    Soul clap hands and sing.

    (Howard University Press library of contemporary literature)

    I. Title.   II. Series.
OS3563.A7223S68   1988   813′.54   88 – 1270
ISBN 0 – 88258 – 155 – 4

The following publishers and authors have generously given permission to use quotations from copyrighted works: From "The Anniad," in *Blacks* by Gwendolyn Brooks. Copyright © 1987 by The David Company, Chicago, Illinois. From the book *Brown Girl, Brownstones.* (The Feminist Press at CUNY), Copyright © 1959 by Paule Marshall. Reprinted with permission. From *The Chosen Place, the Timeless People,* copyright © 1969 by Paule Marshall. Reprinted by permission. Excerpt from "The Hollow Men," in *Collected Poems 1909 – 1962* by T. S. Eliot, copyright © 1936 by Harcourt Brace Jovanovich, Inc., copyright © 1964, 1963 by T. S. Eliot, reprinted by permission of the publisher. Also reprinted by permission of Faber and Faber Ltd from *Collected Poems 1909 – 1962* by T. S. Eliot. From the book *Reena and Other Stories* by Paule Marshall. Copyright © 1983 by The Feminist Press at CUNY. Reprinted with permission.

TO MY SON, EVAN-KEITH

An aged man is but a paltry thing,
A tattered coat upon a stick, unless
Soul clap its hands and sing.

SAILING TO BYZANTIUM
W. B. YEATS

INTRODUCTION

During the summer of 1976 at the University of Iowa, I directed an institute designed to improve research and teaching in Black Studies by comparing Black American culture, experience, and thought from 1845 to 1860 with those elements from 1945 to 1960. The institute provided college and university teachers of Afro-American culture with an opportunity to listen to and communicate with lecturers who were distinguished creators or scholars of that culture. I invited Paule Marshall, who had published her first novel in 1959, to deliver the final lecture of the institute. I asked her to discuss anything that she wished about her experience and intentions as a Black writer of the period 1945 to 1960, and I sent her an institute schedule which listed the titles of the lectures that were to precede hers. Paule Marshall arrived in Iowa City on the morning of the day on which she was to speak. Although she had heard no lectures preceding hers, she delivered a brilliant address in which she commented on topics of the previous lectures, discussed her own writing, and showed how it related to the topics of earlier lectures. She provided the institute participants with a summary of the institute and a conclusion as informed as if she had attended every lecture, taking notes to include in her final presentation. As I rose to join in the standing ovation, I realized that few others in the audience would fully understand how industriously and carefully she had worked to prepare a speech that would meet our needs.

A few years later, the Women's Studies Program invited her to the university. This time, she focused her entire lecture on the manner in which listening to Black women's conversations in her mother's kitchen had contributed to her growth as a writer and a woman. As she continuously emphasized the strength and the significance of Black women, I considered the fact that she earns no headlines as a leader of the feminist movement.

On still another occasion, I brought to the campus a Black American writer who, living abroad, explains that he has little familiarity with the current work of Afro-American writers. While I was awaiting his arrival in the airport, I purchased a paperback copy of Marshall's *The Chosen Place, the Timeless People* (1969). On the way to his hotel, he began to read the novel casually, then more carefully. Finally he stated, "This is a very good writer"; and he asked to keep the book so that he could finish it. Although her skill can immediately impress an internationally known author, Black novelist John McCluskey, Jr. (Mari Evans, ed., *Black Women Writers*, Doubleday, 1984, p. 316) noted with dismay "the relative lack of criticism" of an author who has published three novels—*Brown Girl, Brownstones* (1959); *The Chosen Place, the Timeless People* (1969); *Praisesong for the Widow* (1983)—and two collections of shorter fiction—*Soul Clap Hands and Sing* (1961) and *Reena and Other Stories* (1984).

In fall 1986, I taught Marshall's first novel, *Brown Girl, Brownstones*, to an interracial class of university juniors, seniors, and graduate students examining images of Black women in modern American fiction. Before we discussed the novel, some white women students complained that they found little to excite them in the work; it merely revealed quietly and realistically the way in which a Black girl of West Indian ancestry grows to physical and intellectual maturity in Brooklyn. They were comparing Marshall's novel with fiction by such men as Mark Twain, Jean Toomer, William Faulkner, and Richard Wright and by such women as Zora Neale Hurston and Alice Walker. The students had not always trusted the images of women that these authors created, but the students had found excitement in the apparently more exotic or dramatic or noble portrayals. They began to appreciate Marshall's art, however, after we examined the manner in which she achieves credibility through characterization, plot, dialogue, setting, and local color.

These few anecdotes reveal, in part, the nature of Paule Marshall's work. In her fiction, as in her lectures, she does her homework. That is, she performs her craft so conscientiously, carefully, and thoughtfully that she partially masks the brilliance of her art.

Unlike some writers who compel readers to believe their improbable situations and characters; unlike some writers who dazzle readers with their lyricism; unlike some writers who enchant white readers with the metaphoric quality of Afro-American speech—unlike these writers, Paule Marshall seems to write about Blacks we might have seen living in our neighborhoods, living the kinds of lives we live, speaking a language that we recognize as real, rather than literary.

Marshall develops her themes with the same quiet strength. They do not seem sensational. As McCluskey has observed, her works fit "no neat categorization" as "ornamental eyepieces to a social-political drama . . . [to be judged] on the basis of their accuracy in revealing social tendencies—assimilationist or separatist" (*Black Women Writers at Work*, p. 316). Without militant proclamation or fiery denunciation, Marshall has infused her works with blackness and feminism. She draws her subjects, symbols, traditions, rituals, and language from Black culture throughout the world; and she focuses on—or at least emphasizes—Black women growing in strength as they develop consciousness of themselves.

I

It is sometimes said that a primary motive of Black American creative writers has been to express a reaction to the political, social, and economic issues that have affected Black Americans during the writers' lives. For example, former slave William Wells Brown wrote the novel *Clotel* (1852) to reveal the outrages of slavery. Richard Wright (*Native Son*, 1940) and many others wrote novels in which they demonstrated the psychological effects of racial discrimination and oppression. James Baldwin (*Tell Me How Long the Train's Been Gone*, 1967) and Alice Walker (*Meridian*, 1976) reflected upon the Civil Rights movement of the 1960s. Many writers have even written in response to specific incidents, such as a race riot in Wilmington, North Carolina (Charles Chesnutt) or in Chicago (Claude McKay), the death of Richard Wright and the murder of Malcolm X (John A. Williams), or the lynching of Emmett Till (Gwendolyn Brooks).

If she had chosen to write so topically, Paule Marshall would have had ample material. Born in

Brooklyn, April 9, 1929, on the eve of America's major economic depression, she entered her teenage years while America was engaged in World War II. Before she was twenty-one, America became the first nation to explode an atomic bomb in war. Before she graduated from Brooklyn College (1953), America had been exposed to the traumas of the Dixiecrat* presidential campaign in 1948, the cold war, the Korean War, and McCarthyism.† She graduated from college on the eve of an era, 1954 to 1970, sometimes identified as the "Second Reconstruction" because of the important political and social gains made by Black Americans, who became increasingly determined to gain equality and increasingly optimistic that they could gain their rightful share of the American Dream. In 1954, the United States Supreme Court declared laws to be unconstitutional if they allowed race to be used as a basis for denying Black children admission to public

---

* Reacting against the relatively liberal civil-rights policies of the national Democratic party, which nominated Harry Truman for President, a group of Southern Democrats organized the "Dixiecrat" party, which campaigned as a third party in the presidential election race in 1948.

† Senator Joseph McCarthy of Wisconsin earned national attention—and later infamy—for fanatical efforts to identify and discharge the Communists who, he alleged, were subverting America from their positions in government, the armed services, and other influential sectors. McCarthy's attacks ended after the United States Senate denounced him because he had based destructive "identifications" on rumors or deliberate lies.

schools. Beginning in 1955, Black citizens in the South employed boycotts and protest marches to attack practices of segregation in public transportation; and one year later, the Supreme Court judged the laws of Alabama to be unconstitutional when they required racial segregation on buses. In 1957, the United States Congress passed the first civil rights act since Reconstruction and created the Civil Rights Commission and the Civil Rights Division of the Department of Justice. In 1960, one year after Marshall published her first novel (*Brown Girl, Brownstones*) and one year before *Soul Clap Hands and Sing*, sit-ins throughout the South attacked practices of segregation in public eating places and other public facilities. One year later, the Supreme Court ruled against segregation in interstate transportation; two years after that decision, the Supreme Court declared the segregation laws of Birmingham, Alabama, to be unconstitutional. In that same year, the massive, interracial March on Washington to demand new civil rights laws reached its emotional climax with Martin Luther King, Jr.'s famous "I Have a Dream" speech. In 1964, Congress passed the Civil Rights Act affording Blacks equal access to public facilities; one year later, Congress passed the Voting Rights Act.

These civil rights demonstrations encouraged Americans to turn to works of nonfiction by Black Americans to learn more about their attitudes. Examples of these works are James Baldwin's *Notes of a Native Son* (1955), *Nobody Knows My Name* (1961), and *The Fire Next Time* (1963); Martin Luther King, Jr.'s *Stride Toward Freedom* (1958), *Strength to Love* (1963), *Why We Can't Wait* (1964), and *Where Do We Go From Here: Chaos or Community?* (1967); Alex Haley's *The Autobiography of Malcolm X* (1965); Claude Brown's autobiography, *Manchild in the Promised Land* (1965); and Maya Angelou's first autobiography, *I Know Why the Caged Bird Sings* (1969).

Paule Marshall has not ignored the tumultuous events of her times. Spanning a period from the early years of the depression into the early 1950s, *Brown Girl, Brownstones*, for example, gives attention to a religious movement comparable to that of Father Divine* and notes in passing the manner in which Black women gained opportunities for factory jobs during World War II. In the same novel, she reveals the bitterness that a Black person can feel when bigotry denies recognition of her talent. After a triumphant performance as the only Black in a dance group, Selina Boyce, the protagonist, is infuriated when the mother of another dancer calculatingly ignores Selina's artistry as she recalls how much Selina reminds her

---

* A Black religious leader who reached the zenith of his power during the 1930s. Declaring himself to be God, Father Divine encouraged followers to reject materialism by giving their worldly goods to him so that he might conduct his mission of providing for the hungry and the homeless.

of a former servant. In a masterfully written short story, "Some Get Wasted" (John H. Clarke, ed., *Harlem, U.S.A.*, Seven Seas, 1964; reprinted, New American Library, 1970, pp. 136–45), Marshall narrates the tragic waste of Black leadership potential. Denied an opportunity in the Boy Scouts of America, who nurture only white males, a Black youth turns to the only organization that offers him such experience—the junior division of a neighborhood gang. This potential leader is shot and killed in a war with another gang. In "Brooklyn" (*Soul Clap Hands and Sing*, 1961), a white teacher loses his job because of McCarthy's zealous search for Communists; in *The Chosen Place, the Timeless People* (1969), Merle Kinbona refuses to return to America because it is a land where four young Black girls were killed when white bigots bombed a church that had been used for civil rights meetings.

Despite such reflections of her times, it seems more accurate to say that Paule Marshall inhales the spirit of her times until it becomes a part of her. Then she crafts a narrative which includes the spirit of the times "diastole, systole" (as Robert Hayden wrote in praise of Frederick Douglass's love of liberty). In doing so, she has grown with the spirit of her era and often has anticipated literary themes that would gain greater popularity after her early treatment of them.

During the 1950s when Marshall published her

first stories and her first novel, many Black writers avoided the primary focus on racial or class oppression that had characterized such novels of the 1940s as Wright's *Native Son* (1940), Chester Himes's *If He Hollers Let Him Go* (1945), Ann Petry's *The Street* (1946), and Willard Motley's *Knock on Any Door* (1947). The new writers did not ignore the racial problems of Black Americans. Instead, the writers included the problems among the varied experiences and ideas that shape Black Americans. The writers placed primary emphasis upon exploration of the psychology, attitudes, and culture of Blacks as human beings, rather than on Blacks as oppressed human beings. Quite often, the works clearly suggested how Black Americans, despite some cultural dissimilarities, resemble other Americans in values and in attitudes.

For example, in a focal poem, "The Anniad," from her Pulitzer-Prize-winning *Annie Allen* (Harper, 1949), Gwendolyn Brooks explores the emotions of a young woman who dreams of Prince Charming but marries a more ordinary male; transforms their small apartment into a shrine of love; and loses her husband to the army. When he returns from service, feeling cheated because he has lost years from his youth, he leaves her to seek a more glamorous woman. After she has struggled to reconcile herself to life without him, he returns when he is dying. At twenty-four, "al-

most thoroughly/Derelict and dim and done,"
Annie is left

> Hugging old and Sunday sun.
> Kissing in her kitchenette
> The minuets of memory. (p. 29)

Readers know that Annie is chocolate-brown in
skin color and that her husband's mistress is an
Afro-American of lighter color, but Annie's story
might be that of many women of any race.

Similarly, even though they wrote about Black
protagonists, such authors as Ralph Ellison,
James Baldwin, Louis Peterson, and Lorraine
Hansberry—who preceded Marshall in the
1950s—addressed national and universal questions. Following his exposé of dehumanization of
Americans by American institutions, the Black
narrator-protagonist of *Invisible Man* (1952) asks
his white readers, "Who knows but that, on the
lower frequencies, I speak for you?" (Random
House, p. 439). Certainly, racial bigotry and
oppression affect all of the Black adults in *Go Tell
It on the Mountain* (1952), but Baldwin focuses
on the question of what draws people into a Chris-
tian church. Even though major problems of the
Black teen-aged protagonist in Louis Peterson's
drama *Take a Giant Step* (1953) result from a
white teacher's bigotry and are intensified by the
bigotry of white neighbors, the drama emphasizes
problems common to male youths seeking maturity. Although audiences responded to the sen-

sational issue of white neighborhood opposition to Black residents, Hansberry's *A Raisin in the Sun* (Random House, 1959) concentrates primarily on the aspirations of a woman and her two adult children. The drama, in fact, emphasizes how similar the Black Younger family is to the white Americans who fear their becoming neighbors: "not rich and fancy people; just hard-working, honest people who don't really have much but those little homes and a dream of the kind of community they want to raise their children in (p. 105)."

In *Brown Girl, Brownstones* (1959), similarly, Marshall tells the story of a Black family whose problems are not uniquely those of Black Americans. The mother, Serena Boyce, has come to America in search of the American Dream: through hard work, discipline, and frugal management, she and her family will acquire property, respectability, and a new home. Her immigrant husband, Deighton Boyce, however, wants only to earn enough money to be able to return to his homeland, where he can flaunt his affluence before his neighbors. Torn between the values of these two, their daughter Selina must also experience the problems of a young woman growing to physical, intellectual, psychological, and cultural maturity.

In her focus on Selina's growth, Marshall seems to anticipate *bildungsromans* of Black women.

That is, despite a few notable exceptions, such as Zora Neale Hurston in *Their Eyes Were Watching God* (1937), most Black women authors who wrote about Black women protagonists before 1950 concentrated on their adult lives. Even in *The Street* (1946), Ann Petry sketched only enough of Lutie Johnson's early life to enable a reader to learn something about her values, their source, and her reason for an early marriage. Four years after *Brown Girl, Brownstones*, Mary Elizabeth Vroman, in *Esther* (1963), revealed her protagonist's intellectual and emotional development from the age of thirteen into her adult life. In *God Bless the Child* (1964), Kristin Hunter portrayed Rosie Fleming from the age of seven until her death as a young woman. In the 1980s, when readers familiar with Black literature automatically think of such novels as Toni Morrison's *Sula* (1974) or Alice Walker's *The Color Purple* (1982), a story exploring the maturing of a Black woman does not seem unusual. In 1959, however, Marshall was among the earliest to trace such development.

As she anticipated *bildungsromans* of women, so, even in her first novel, she propounded a theme that others would echo more vociferously throughout the 1960s—the questioning of the value of the American Dream if it is defined by materialism and promoted by ruthless exploitation and destruction of other human beings. Marshall certainly was not the first to treat the theme.

Even though Frank Yerby, in the late 1940s and 1950s, seemed to glamorize the American Dream in his novels about white protagonists who crawled from their positions as impoverished outcasts to luxurious stations as wealthy insiders in nineteenth-century societies of the American South, Yerby stated his conviction that such success resulted not from good character but from a ruthless willingness to exploit others. Ann Petry, in *The Street*, delineated a Black woman who fails in her quest for the dream that she has patterned after the materialistic success of her immoral and unhappy white employers. After Marshall, such Blacks as Baldwin and Malcolm X in the early 1960s denounced the individualism, materialism, and greed of the American Dream in tones that were intensified later in the decade by writers of the Black Arts movement.

In the novellas of *Soul Clap Hands and Sing* (1961), Marshall continued to adumbrate particular themes that embody or anticipate the spirit of her era. Although it takes place outside the United States of America, "Barbados" suggests the potential pathetic fate of a man who surrenders his humanity to the materialism of the American Dream. "Brazil" explores the traumas of the quest to define one's identity and to live according to the dictates of that real identity, that real self, rather than to live behind a mask. In *Brown Girl, Brownstones*, Selina struggles to learn who she is, what she wants. Although it was not new in Western literature, this theme became dominant in Afro-American literature of the 1960s as Black writers attempted to define themselves and their race. In *Soul Clap Hands and Sing*, Marshall continued to describe women's growth into a confident consciousness of self. Marshall does not explore this issue as colorfully as Hurston does in *Their Eyes Were Watching God* (1937), as dramatically as Alice Walker does in *The Color Purple* (1982), or even as overtly as she herself would in *Praisesong for the Widow* (1983). Nevertheless, this theme is fundamental to the book.

Finally, Marshall suggests the significance of cultural nationalism, of allegiance to cultural ancestry. In *Brown Girl, Brownstones*, after rejecting the provinciality and elitism of the Barbadian Association, Selina decides to visit the West Indies to learn about her ancestry first-hand. In *Soul Clap Hands and Sing*, Marshall, having written about West Indians living in the U.S.A., focused on West Indians and South Americans living in their own lands. A muted issue during the 1950s, when many Afro-American writers affirmed the homogeneity of Americans, the emphasis upon pride in cultural ancestry, pride in one's roots became the 1960s' clarion call that reached its zenith in Alex Haley's *Roots* (1977).

The decade after *Brown Girl, Brownstones* proved so fertile for Afro-American literature that it has sometimes been identified as the "Second Renaissance." Just as publishers solicited the kinds of nonfiction noted earlier, so they sought fiction, drama, and poetry by Black writers.

Lorraine Hansberry's *A Raisin in the Sun* (1959), which has had the longest run on Broadway of any play written by a Black, and LeRoi Jones's *Dutchman* (1963) earned critics' awards early in the decade. In 1965, a group of critics and authors selected Ralph Ellison's *Invisible Man* (1952) as the most distinguished American novel since World War II. By the end of the decade, Lonne Elder's *Ceremonies in Dark Old Men* (1968) had been nominated for a Pulitzer Prize in drama, and Charles Gordone's *No Place to Be Somebody* (1969) had won one.

Possibly inspired by the political and social ferment or by the interest of publishers and the reading public, Black dramatists, poets, and fiction writers who are well known in the 1980s made their debuts in the 1960s. Johara Amini, Ed Bullins, Lonne Elder, Mari Evans, Sarah Fabio, Nikki Giovanni, Charles Gordone, LeRoi Jones, Audrey Lorde, Etheridge Knight, Don L. Lee, Marvin X, Larry Neal, Conrad Kent Rivers, Sonia Sanchez, and Douglas Turner Ward comprise a representative list of well-known Black poets and dramatists who published their first books in the 1960s.*

---

* Jones later changed his name to Amiri Baraka, and Don L. Lee changed his to Haki R. Madhubuti.

Black fiction writers experience greater difficulty attaining exposure than do poets and dramatists. Blacks may produce their dramas through
Black amateur, semi-professional, or professional
theatrical groups; many of these groups devel-
oped during the 1960s. If they compile small collections of poetry, Black writers may absorb the
cost of publication themselves; or they may find
outlets through underfinanced Black publishers,
such as Broadside Press or Third World Press. For
a novel or a collection of short stories, however,
a Black writer, more often than not, must depend
upon a large commercial publisher that has a
budget adequate to cover the cost of publication
and distribution. (This series of reprints by Howard University Press attempts to ease the problem.) Despite this economic restriction, a signif-
icant number of well-known Black writers
published their first novels shortly before or during the 1960s.

In 1961, the year in which *Soul Clap Hands
and Sing* appeared, Julian Mayfield, author of *The
Hit* (1957) and *The Long Night* (1958), produced
his third novel, *The Grand Parade*; and John A.
Williams followed his first novel, *The Angry Ones*
(1960), with *Night Song*. After 1961, the number
of Black novelists grew rapidly: Barry Beckham,
Hal Bennett, Robert Boles, Junius Edwards, Ron-
ald Fair, Rosa Guy, Clarence Major, Gordon
Parks, Charles Perry, Carlene Hatcher Polite, Ish-
mael Reed, Henry Van Dyke, Melvin Van Pee-

bles, Mary Elizabeth Vroman, Margaret Walker (published earlier as a poet), John Edgar Wideman, Charles Wright, and Sarah Wright. This abbreviated list of Black writers who published their first books of fiction during the 1960s approximately doubles the number of Black Americans who published their first books of fiction during the highly acclaimed Renaissance of the 1920s.

Marshall's fiction after *Soul Clap Hands and Sing* must be examined in relation to the work of these new dramatists, poets, and novelists who emerged during the 1960s.

If one examines the work of Afro-American fiction writers, poets, and dramatists from 1954 to 1970, one perceives two groups, both dedicated to improving the status of Blacks within the U.S.A. One group continued in the tradition that most Black American writers had practiced since the eighteenth century: They sought to improve the condition of Blacks by writing to the majority reading audience of America (by definition, a white audience) in order (1) to win sympathy or support by educating the reading public to comprehend the needs and aspirations of Black Americans; or (2) to win respect for Afro-Americans by demonstrating their own artistic ability to excel when judged according to the criteria of the literary establishment (the most respected white critics and scholars). This group, which might be called "traditionalists" for lack of a better term, did not wish to "bleach its Blackness" (to quote Du Bois) in order to assimilate into American society. Many writers in the group, in fact, denounced bigotry and the falseness of the American Dream in strident and militant tones. Nevertheless, they continued the traditional practices. A few traditionalists who emerged between 1954 and 1970 are LeRoi Jones* and Conrad Kent Rivers in poetry; James Baldwin, Julian Mayfield, John A. Williams, and Kristin Hunter in fiction; Lorraine Hansberry and Baldwin and Jones in drama.

A second group of Black writers and critics, primarily those who began to publish poetry and drama after 1963, argued that it was futile to attempt to improve the Black American condition by educating white Americans or by trying to prove Black artistic excellence. Instead, this group, often called "Black Arts writers and critics," insisted that Blacks should write according to a Black aesthetic and should direct themselves only to Black audiences. Moreover, they argued that Black writers should use only Black subjects, Black consciousness, Black themes, Black style, Black language, Black customs, and Black settings to educate Black audiences to the need for liberating themselves from white domination. Fi-

* Jones later became a leader in the Black Arts movement.

nally, Black Arts writers insisted that these works should be evaluated only by critics sympathetic to the Black Arts movement. Some of these writers are Amiri Baraka, Haki R. Madhubuti, and Sonia Sanchez in poetry; Baraka and Ed Bullins in drama; and John Killens in the novel.

Obviously, this simplified categorization does not provide a place for all writers. For example, poet and novelist Gwendolyn Brooks associated with and influenced Black Arts poets; rejecting opportunities with white publishers, she published her later poetry through Broadside Press, a small Black-owned firm that distributes its books primarily among Black audiences. On the other hand, Nikki Giovanni, whose early poetry evidences the Black Arts movement, chose to distribute her later work only through large commercial publishing houses.

Without taking allegiance with either the traditionalists or the Black Arts writers, Paule Marshall imbibed the exhilarating spirits of both groups and distilled them into a literature that exudes the spirit of the era. In her second novel, *The Chosen Place, the Timeless People* (1969), she wrote for the majority audience, but she focused on a theme pleasing to Black Arts writers— the struggle of Merle Kinbona to preserve the customs and the traditions of her homeland against the wealthy Black West Indians and white Americans who would transform that island with U.S. American values and technology.

The difficulty of categorizing Marshall's work is evidenced further by *Praisesong for the Widow* (1983). Despite the fact that Marshall has had so little identification with the Black Arts movement that John Killens, a Black Arts proponent, even seemed to mock *Brown Girl, Brownstones* (1959) in his novel *The Cotillion* (1971), *Praisesong for the Widow*, I believe, is a Black Arts/Black Aesthetic novel without the violence and obscenity that some readers presume essential to such a work. Having dreamed of fighting against her grandaunt Cuney, who urged her to return to the family home on Tatem Island (South Carolina), sixty-two-year-old Avey (Avatara) Johnson abruptly abandons her cruise through the West Indies. As she returns to Grenada to await a plane to New York, she is haunted by memories of her late husband. She recalls their life on Halsey Street in Brooklyn before 1945—a life in which they were desperately poor financially but wealthy in their enjoyment of love, dancing, Black culture, and the Black community. She also recalls how her threat to leave him—a threat provoked by poverty and unwarranted jealousy—transformed him into a person who diminished their humanity and severed their association with Black culture and community as he obsessively drove himself in pursuit of the materialistic dream.

In Grenada, Avey Johnson meets the ancient Lebert Joseph (Papa Legba), who encourages her to accompany him and other out-islanders on their annual excursion to their home on the island of Carriacou. Purging her materialism, the journey re-establishes her communion with African tradition and the Black community. Comprehending the significance of her name "Avatara" (incarnation of a deity or embodiment of a spirit), she decides to sell her home in North White Plains, New York, so that she can spend at least six months each year on Tatem, where she will teach her grandsons the story of the Ibos, who, having envisioned the horror of their lives in the land to which they had been taken in chains, walked back across the Atlantic Ocean to Africa.

The novel does not merely evidence the spirit of Black Arts literature by focusing on a Black subject, by emphasizing the liberating qualities of the themes, by affirming the importance of community and tradition, and by depicting a knowledgeable Black (a true revolutionary, Papa Legba) who educates a younger Black, Johnson, to awareness. The novel also reflects the "saturation" of blackness that Stephen Henderson (*Understanding the New Black Poetry*, 1972) insists is essential to a definition of "Black" poetry—and, by extension, "Black" literature. That is, seeking metaphors and allusions, the writer instinctively draws them from Black culture, rather than from Anglo-European culture. In such manner, Marshall depicts Jay and Avey Johnson as they quote poetry of Langston Hughes, James Weldon Johnson, and Paul Laurence Dunbar; listen to the music of Duke Ellington, Count Basie, and Coleman Hawkins or to the songs of Ella Fitzgerald or Billie Holiday; or dance to "Take the A-Train" or "Stompin' at the Savoy." The novel's stories and legends are African and Afro-American. The dances and the songs during the excursion to Carriacou are Afro-Caribbean and African. In short, the novel brilliantly illustrates the manner in which a writer may incorporate the essential blackness of a Black Aesthetic and Black Arts without stressing an ideology that may alienate some readers.

In summary, from 1959 to 1983, Marshall created a series of novels and short stories that reflect the spirit of her times. Fundamental in this revelation of the spirit is Marshall's interest in Black women's growth and in cultural nationalism.

II

A staff writer for *Our World* magazine (1953–56), a lecturer and professor at such universities as Columbia, Fisk, Yale, and Iowa, Paule Marshall, in her career as a fiction writer, has remained faithful to particular techniques and convictions. She has achieved credibility in characterization and in theme partly by comprehending and presenting the total complexity of people and issues. In *Brown Girl, Brownstones* (1959), for example, the characters who help Selina learn about life are neither heroines, heroes, nor villains. They are people who have strengths and virtues. Selina's mother, Silla, may seem to be so obsessively devoted to the materialism of the American Dream that she will destroy anyone who thwarts her goal; but Marshall reminds us of Silla's passionate love for her husband, Deighton, and of her love for her children. When Deighton, angered by his wife's selling the land that he inherited, spends the entire $900 for gifts for her and for the children, Silla wails, "Oh, Lord-God . . . I was gon buy them things. . . . I was gon buy them as soon as I did catch muh hand. . . . I know they's girls and does like pretty things. . ." (p. 133). On first examination, Deighton may seem more charming, more likable than Silla. He is a romantic dreamer who seems to have escaped the trap of materialism. He is, however, almost as ruthless as Silla in securing vengeance; and he does desire affluence even though he is not as willing as Silla to sacrifice himself to acquire it. The complexity of Selina, the protagonist, enables readers to perceive positive possibilities in what seemed to be the weaknesses of her parents. Although Selina rebels against her mother, whom

she calls "Hitler," and sympathizes with her father's dreams, her boyfriend, Clive, advises her
that she is more like her mother than she suspects.
Readers learn this truth when Selina finally rec-
ognizes how Silla's strength supports the family.
Eventually, just as Silla argued against Deighton's weakness, so Selina, in her turn, abandons
her boyfriend because he is too weak.

Issues too are complex. In "To Da-Duh, In Me-
moriam" (1967, reprinted in *Reena and Other
Stories*, Feminist Press, 1984, pp. 93–106), a story
based on Marshall's memory of her grandmother,
an American girl visiting her grandmother in Barbados competes with the woman as they compare
cultures. Readers perceive the garishness and
brassiness of the girl's examples of American culture—Tin Pan Alley songs and "Trucking"
dances—in comparison with the grandmother's
examples from nature and tradition. However, the
grandmother seems to lose confidence in her culture each time the girl cites a new example. Finally, the grandmother surrenders after her boast
that New York has nothing as large as a palm tree
is dwarfed by the girl's description of New York's
skyscrapers. Captivated by the girl's tales, the
grandmother no longer observes nature; her vision has been obstructed by "some huge mono-
lithic shape" (p. 105). After the girl has returned
to New York, the grandmother dies, apparently
while watching airplanes invade the Barbadian

skies. The triumph of the machines, however, saddens the girl, who continues to live within the shadow of the grandmother's death and who, as an adult, paints "seas of sugar-cane and huge swirling Van Gogh suns and palm trees" (p. 106), despite the mocking thunder of the machines in the factory beneath her loft.

The complexity of issues can be perceived also in *The Chosen Place, the Timeless People* (1969). Even though readers are glad that Merle and "the Little Fella" have successfully defeated the "machines" of American science, readers also perceive that implementation of some of the American plans would benefit the people of Bournehills.

Her presentation of people and issues probably reflects Marshall's absorption of the philosophy that she learned from her mother and her mother's friends. In "From the Poets in the Kitchen" (*Reena and Other Stories*, p. 9), Marshall explains that her mother and her friends believed that "a thing is at the same time its opposite, and that these opposites, the contradictions make up the whole" (p. 9).

While remaining faithful to particular techniques and convictions, Marshall has grown more bold as an artist, daring to rise from the realistic to the mythic in her descriptions and characterizations. In *Brown Girl, Brownstones* (1959), she described the ever-threatening machines realistically. At most, the scene becomes surrealistic:

Cautiously Selina walked down the long corridor, her footsteps accompanying her until they
merged with an ominous current of sound.
Timidly she pushed open a heavy metal door
and almost slammed it back in fright as an enraged bellow tore past her. She was drowned
suddenly in a deluge of noise: belts slapping
on giant pulleys, long shafts rearing and plunging, whirling parts plying the air, the metal
whine of steel being cut, steam hissing from a
twisting network of pipes on the ceilings and
walls, the nervous, high-strung hum of the
smaller machines and finally the relentless
frightening stamp of the larger ones, which
made the floor shudder. It was a controlled,
mechanical hysteria, welling up like a seething
volcano to the point of eruption, only to veer
off at the climax and start again.

And just as the noise of each machine had
been welded into a single howl, so did the
machines themselves seem forged into one
sprawling, colossal machine. This machine-
mass, this machine-force was ugly, yet it had
grandeur. It was a new creative force, the heart
of another, larger, form of life that had submerged all others, and the roar was its heart-
beat—not the ordered systole and diastole of
the human heart but a frenetic lifebeat all its
own.

The workers, white and colored, clustered
and scurried around the machine-mass, trying,
it seemed, to stave off the destruction it threatened. They had built it but, ironically, it had
overreached them, so that now they were only
small insignificant shapes against its over-

whelming complexity. Their movements mim-
icked its mechanical gestures. They pulled
levers, turned wheels, scooped up the metal
droppings of the machines as if somewhere in
that huge building someone controlled their
every motion by pushing a button. And no one
talked. Like the men loading the trailer trucks
in the streets, they performed a pantomime role
in a drama in which only the machines had a
voice. (pp. 98–99)

Eventually, of course, such monstrous machines
cripple Selina's father.

In *The Chosen Place, the Timeless People*
(1969), the triumph of the machines seems almost
mythic. Having studied books about automobiles,
Vere, with loving care and patience, has con-
structed his own and has entered a race:

The Opel . . . was outperforming all the cars
he had driven in the dream. It responded to his
slightest touch, the months of hard work he had
put into restoring it. Moreover, as his foot bore
steadily down on the accelerator and the speed
began to build under him, he felt the combined
power of that supercharged German motor and
long, low-slung American body which, in
motion, looked like an animal lunging forward
to strike, flow up through the floor and through
the shaft of the steering wheel and enter him,
becoming his power. His smile widening, he
spurred the Opel ahead, and the surprised roar
that went up as he took the lead and left the
other cars scrambling in the dust behind, was
the same stunning hosanna of his imagining, a
sound like the roaring of his own blood in his
ears. . . .

He was more than halfway to Westminster, the race his (the crowd was already proclaiming him the undisputed winner) when he felt the first tremor. It was like a horse grown restive under too tight a rein, and treating it accordingly, he eased up a little on the pedal, still smiling to himself. And his smile—that beautiful but too trusting Vere smile which was like a light illumining his face—held even when the first of what was to be a series of massive shudders began deep in the chassis and, quickly spreading up, shook the entire frame. His foot shifted then from the gas to the brake pedal only to find—and here his expression took on a slight note of surprise—that although he was pressing it all the way to the floor nothing happened; the brake did not hold.

With that the car seemed to fall completely apart around him, disintegrating, all of it, into so many separate parts, the wheels moving out from their axle, the steering device becoming unhinged from its mooring under the dashboard, all the bolts and nuts and screws which he had so painstakingly and with such love secured over the months coming loose at once. The collapse was so total it seemed deliberate, planned, personally intended. It was as if the Opel, though only a machine, had possessed a mind, an intelligence, that for some reason had remained unalterably opposed to Vere, so that while doing his bidding and permitting him to think he was making it over into his own image, to express him, it had also at the same time been conspiring against him and waiting coolly for this moment to show its hand.

Or perhaps it had nothing to do with Vere. The collapse taking place around him, which

he was helpless to stop, flowed perhaps out of
a profoundly self-destructive impulse within
the machine itself, and Vere, in foolishly allow-
ing himself to be taken in by what he had
believed was its promise of power, was simply
a hapless victim. (pp. 392–93)

As she has risen to the mythic in description of
nonhuman forces, so she has elevated her characters from the complex reality of those in *Brown
Girl, Brownstones* to the grandeur of Merle Kinbona in *The Chosen Place, the Timeless People*.
In *Reena and Other Stories* (1984), Marshall herself has provided the best description of Merle:

> "Part saint, part revolutionary, part obeah
> woman"—obeah meaning juju, mojo, magic,
> someone who possesses magical powers. That
> was the way one reviewer described Merle
> Kinbona, the black woman who is the central
> figure in *The Chosen Place, the Timeless
> People*. It's an apt description, for it suggests
> the several ways I wanted her to function in
> the story.
>   Merle remains the most alive of my charac-
> ters. Indeed, it seems to me she has escaped
> the pages of the novel altogether and is abroad
> in the world. I envision her striding restlessly
> up and down the hemisphere from Argentina to
> Canada, and back and forth across the Atlantic
> between here and Africa, all the while speak-
> ing her mind in the same forthright way as in
> the book. She can be heard condemning all
> forms of exploitation, injustice and greed. In El
> Salvador, Harlem, Haiti, at the Plaza de Mayo

in Buenos Aires and amid the favelas of Rio de
Janeiro, wherever she goes, she continues to
exhort "the little Fella" as she calls the poor
and oppressed to resist, to organize, to rise up
against the condition of their lives. Like Gan-
dhi, she considers poverty the greatest violence
that can be done a people. I hear her inveigh-
ing constantly against the arms race, the Bomb,
against a technology run amok: "Everything . . .
gone from the face of the earth . . . The silence!
You can hear a pin drop the world over. Everybody gone . . ."

On a personal level, she's still trying to come
to terms with her life and history as a black
woman, still seeking to reconcile all the con-
flicting elements to form a viable self. And she
continues to search, as in the novel, for the
kind of work, for a role in life, that will put to
use her tremendous energies and talent. Merle.
She's the most passionate and political of my
heroines. A Third World revolutionary spirit.
And I love her. (p. 109)

In *Praisesong for the Widow* (1983), Marshall's
characterizations approach and attain mythic lev-
els without losing the credibility of their human-
ness. Avey Johnson transcends her middle-class,
self-centered identity to rise to her new identity
as Avatara, the embodiment of the spirit of the
deity. In this identity, she will teach new gen-
erations the lessons that she has learned from
grandaunt Cuney and from Lebert Joseph, the incarnation of the African deity Papa Legba. She
will teach with special love the story of the mythic
Ibos.

A second major lesson that Avey Johnson has learned from her experience on Grenada and Carriacou is the importance of the community. The theme appeared in Marshall's earlier work. Silla Boyce strengthened herself by immersion in the community of Barbadian women in her neighborhood and by participation in the Barbadian Association. Deighton Boyce found strength in the community nurtured by Father Peace. Although Selina resists identification with the organizations that support her parents, she establishes her own community of Beryl, Suggie, Mrs. Thompson, Clive, and others who help her mature. In *The Chosen Place, the Timeless People*, Merle Kinbona defined herself as isolated, an exile; but she attempted to defend and support the poor people of Bournehills, "the little Fella." Marshall emphasized the theme even more, however, in *Praisesong for the Widow*. Despite their affluence, Jerome and Avey Johnson lose an important part of themselves when they move into North White Plains and end their visits to Tatem Island, alienating themselves from the Black community. Avey even fights when her dead grandaunt, in a dream, tries to persuade her to return to Tatem. On Grenada, Avey Johnson learns of the "out-islanders," whose strength is their community and their preservation of tradition. Joining their ritualistic excursion, Avey learns the importance of such strength, and she vows to gain her own strength by returning to Tatem Island and to its traditions.

By 1983, almost twenty-five years since her first novel appeared, Marshall had grown from realistic depiction to mythic presentation. Simultaneously, she heightened her emphasis on the intellectual growth of women and on the importance of a Black individual's bond to a Black community.

III

When *Soul Clap Hands and Sing* appeared in 1961, Marshall had not reached that level of 1983. Readers of the work should look for two motifs that Marshall has explained:

> The four long stories which make up the collection all have to do with old men. They are—the men—of different backgrounds and cultures, yet they share a common predicament: their lives have been essentially empty. They have failed to commit themselves to anyone or anything in a meaningful way. When confronted with this truth or when their long-suppressed need for love finally surfaces, they reach out in a desperate, last-ditch effort to the women in the stories. (While the women are not major characters, they are nonetheless important as "bringers of the truth," and also because they come to realize their own strength as a result of the encounter. I saw this as a second motif.)

> One of the reasons I undertook *Soul Clap
> Hands and Sing* was to see if I could write con-
> vincingly of men. More important, I wanted to
> use the relationships between the old men and
> the young women in the stories to suggest
> themes of a political nature. These were of in-
> creasing interest to me at the time (*Reena and
> Other Stories*, 1984, p. 51).

Anyone who has read to this point in this introduction will not be surprised to learn that one
motif is the manner in which women grow in consciousness. Years before Black women became
identified with the feminist movement, Marshall
articulated themes now identified with that
movement. Marshall has described the development of the serving girl in "Barbados": "She
evolves from a silent, submerged, anonymous
creature into a young woman with a growing
sense of herself and her rights" (p. 52). Marshall's
words characterize also the young Black woman
in "Brooklyn," who evolves from a shy, insecure
student into a woman able to perceive her su-
periority to her instructor. In the other two novellas, one should perceive women's strength: In
"British Guiana," a woman risks security to gamble for success; in "Brazil," a stage performer re-
tains awareness of her identity, never confusing
it with her role on the stage.

Readers of *Soul Clap Hands and Sing*, however, must also examine closely the primary
motif—the old men who are the protagonists.

These men belong to no community and honor no traditions. They are the hollow men of whom T. S. Eliot wrote:

> We are the hollow men
> We are the stuffed men
> Leaning together
> Headpiece filled with straw. Alas!
> Our dried voices, when
> We whisper together
> Are quiet and meaningless
> As wind in dry grass
> Or rats' feet over broken glass
> In our dry cellar
>
> Shape without form, shade without color,
> Paralyzed force, gesture without motion;
>
> Those who have crossed
> With direct eyes, to death's other Kingdom
> Remember us—if at all—not as lost
> Violent souls, but only
> As the hollow men
> The stuffed men.

> (T. S. Eliot, *The Complete Poems and Plays, 1909–1950*, Harcourt, Brace, and World, 1962, p. 56)

These are the protagonists: A wealthy, retired man who fears to surrender to people and to passion; an aging teacher who has lost his Jewish faith and who never fully accepted communism or teaching as a replacement; a BBC manager who has succumbed into the unchallenging security of his ineffectual job; an aging entertainer who has gained fame but has lost his identity.

The stories of these men illustrate the timeliness and the universality of art. These males reflect the weaknesses that Greek artists of the fifth century before Christ posited for their tragic heroes, and they embody the weaknesses of tragic modern man. The Greek philosopher Aristotle explained that the ideal hero of a tragedy was basically a virtuous person weakened by a tragic flaw—generally an obsession. Material wealth, security, fame: These obsessions govern Marshall's male protagonists, who sacrifice human companionship in order to pursue their dreams. Simultaneously, however, Marshall has illustrated the tragedy of modern man, who suffers from loneliness and uncertainty of his identity. The tragedy, Marshall suggests, does not limit itself to one race or country; it affects all Western males.

At the risk of seeming to substitute informality for scholarly detachment, I began this introduction with personal anecdotes about Paule Marshall. In similar manner, I must conclude with a reflection. When I reread these novellas in preparation for writing an introduction, I was startled to discover that I sympathized with the protagonists less than I had when I first read the collection. Knowing that, if anything, I respected Marshall's artistry more than I had two and one-half decades earlier, I probed the causes of my new reaction and discovered that the difference resided in me, not in Marshall's art.

When I first read these novellas, the protagonists haunted me: a man who, obsessed with wealth, misses his chance for love and companionship; a man who cannot sublimate his physical need for human companionship into intellectual flirtations with religion, culture, and political ideology; a man who slides into dull mediocrity because he fears to gamble with life. Most of all, I was haunted by that protagonist whose success and fame created an image so awe-inspiring that admirers could no longer recognize the actual man. For me, these were ghosts of the future that a Paule Marshall, rather than a Charles Dickens, had created as warnings to young male professionals. Like Aristotelian tragic heroes, these protagonists were intended to effect a katharsis through sympathy and fear. We readers should sympathize with them, and we should fear that we might plunge into such tragic destinies unless we subdue our obsessions. I responded personally, individually identifying with each protagonist.

When I reread the novellas to prepare for this introduction, one-quarter of a century had passed. I had entered the generation of the protagonists. They no longer seemed to be horrifying ghosts of the future; they were ghosts of the past and present—pallid images I had perceived in people whom I had known or echoes of people about whom I had read: a ghost-like President of the United States who wandered alone in the midnight halls of the White House; a multi-billionaire who died alone in his germ-free room; an actress who killed herself, possibly because her image blinded admirers to the insecurity of her real person; a professor who thought that a honeymoon meant taking his work to the beach rather than to his study.

Now, because I am part of that generation and because my experiences have forced me to perceive the loneliness and the obsession of real people near the ends of their careers, I view the protagonists with greater familiarity. Rather than judging them to be horrifying exceptions to the human condition, I nod regretfully as I recognize the shadows of friends and colleagues.

This, I believe, is a major dimension of Paule Marshall's art in *Soul Clap Hands and Sing.* She has created protagonists who are so true that readers comprehend them more fully as the readers become more perceptive about the weaknesses of human beings.

> *Darwin T. Turner*
> University of Iowa
> May 1988

CONTENTS

Barbados   3

Brooklyn   31

British Guiana   67

Brazil   131

BARBADOS

Dawn, like the night which

had preceded it, came from the sea. In a white mist tumbling like spume over the fishing boats leaving the island and the hunched, ghost shapes of the fishermen. In a white, wet wind breathing over the villages scattered amid the tall canes. The cabbage palms roused, their high headdresses solemnly saluting the wind, and along the white beach which ringed the island the casuarina trees began their moaning—a sound of women lamenting their dead within a cave.

The wind, smarting of the sea, threaded a wet skein through Mr. Watford's five hundred dwarf coconut trees and around his house at the edge of the grove. The house, Colonial American in design, seemed created by the mist—as if out of the dawn's formlessness had come, magically, the solid stone walls, the blind, broad windows and the portico of fat columns which embraced the main story. When the mist cleared, the house remained —pure, proud, a pristine white—disdaining the crude wooden houses in the village outside its high gate.

It was not the dawn settling around his house which awakened Mr. Watford, but the call of his

Barbary doves from their hutch in the yard. And it was more the feel of that sound than the sound itself. His hands had retained, from the many times a day he held the doves, the feel of their throats swelling with that murmurous, mournful note. He lay abed now, his hands—as cracked and calloused as a cane cutter's—filled with the sound, and against the white sheet which flowed out to the white walls he appeared profoundly alone, yet secure in loneliness, contained. His face was fleshless and severe, his black skin sucked deep into the hollow of his jaw, while under a high brow, which was like a bastion raised against the world, his eyes were indrawn and pure. It was as if during all his seventy years, Mr. Watford had permitted nothing to sight which could have affected him.

He stood up, and his body, muscular but stripped of flesh, appeared to be absolved from time, still young. Yet each clenched gesture of his arms, of his lean shank as he dressed in a faded shirt and work pants, each vigilant, snapping motion of his head betrayed tension. Ruthlessly he spurred his body to perform like a younger man's. Savagely he denied the accumulated fatigue of the years. Only sometimes when he paused in his grove of coconut trees during the day, his eyes tearing and the breath torn from his lungs, did it seem that if he could find a place hidden from the world and himself he would give way to exhaustion and weep from weariness.

Dressed, he strode through the house, his step tense, his rough hand touching the furniture from Grand Rapids which crowded each room. For some reason, Mr. Watford had never completed the house. Everywhere the walls were raw and unpainted, the furniture unarranged. In the drawing room with its coffered ceiling, he stood before his favorite piece, an old mantel clock which eked out the time. Reluctantly it whirred five and Mr. Watford nodded. His day had begun.

It was no different from all the days which made up the five years since his return to Barbados. Downstairs in the unfinished kitchen, he prepared his morning tea—tea with canned milk and fried bakes—and ate standing at the stove while lizards skittered over the unplastered walls. Then, belching and snuffling the way a child would, he put on a pith helmet, secured his pants legs with bicycle clasps and stepped into the yard. There he fed the doves, holding them so that their sound poured into his hands and laughing gently—but the laugh gave way to an irritable grunt as he saw the mongoose tracks under the hutch. He set the trap again.

The first heat had swept the island like a huge tidal wave when Mr. Watford, with that tense, headlong stride, entered the grove. He had planted the dwarf coconut trees because of their quick yield and because, with their stunted trunks, they always appeared young. Now as he worked, rearranging the complex of pipes which irrigated the land, stripping off the dead leaves, the trees were like cool, moving presences; the stiletto fronds wove a protective dome above him and slowly, as the day soared toward noon, his mind filled with the slivers of sunlight through the trees and the feel of earth in his hands, as it might have been filled with thoughts.

Except for a meal at noon, he remained in the grove until dusk surged up from the sea; then returning to the house, he bathed and dressed in a medical doctor's white uniform, turned on the lights in the parlor and opened the tall doors to the portico. Then the old women of the village on their way to church, the last hawkers caroling, "Fish, flying fish, a penny, my lady," the roistering saga-boys lugging their heavy steel drums to the crossroad where they would rehearse under the street lamp—all passing could glimpse Mr. Watford, stiff in his white uniform and with his head bent heavily over a Boston newspaper. The papers reached him weeks late but he read them anyway, giving a little savage chuckle at the thought that beyond his world that other world went its senseless way. As he read, the night sounds of the village welled into a joyous chorale against the sea's muffled cadence and the hollow, haunting music of the steel band. Soon the moths, lured in by the light, fought to die on the lamp, the beetles crashed drunkenly against the walls and the night

—like a woman offering herself to him—became fragrant with the night-blooming cactus.

Even in America Mr. Watford had spent his evenings this way. Coming home from the hospital, where he worked in the boiler room, he would dress in his white uniform and read in the basement of the large rooming house he owned. He had lived closeted like this, detached, because America—despite the money and property he had slowly accumulated—had meant nothing to him. Each morning, walking to the hospital along the rutted Boston streets, through the smoky dawn light, he had known—although it had never been a thought—that his allegience, his place, lay elsewhere. Neither had the few acquaintances he had made mattered. Nor the women he had occasionally kept as a younger man. After the first months their bodies would grow coarse to his hand and he would begin edging away. . . . So that he had felt no regret when, the year before his retirement, he resigned his job, liquidated his properties and, his fifty-year exile over, returned home.

The clock doled out eight and Mr. Watford folded the newspaper and brushed the burnt moths from the lamp base. His lips still shaped the last words he had read as he moved through the rooms, fastening the windows against the night air, which he had dreaded even as a boy. Something palpable but unseen was always, he believed, crouched in the night's dim recess, waiting to snare him. . . .

Once in bed in his sealed room, Mr. Watford fell asleep quickly.

The next day was no different except that Mr. Goodman, the local shopkeeper, sent the boy for coconuts to sell at the race track and then came that evening to pay for them and to herald—although Mr. Watford did not know this—the coming of the girl.

That morning, taking his tea, Mr. Watford heard the careful tap of the mule's hoofs and looking out saw the wagon jolting through the dawn and the boy, still lax with sleep, swaying on the seat. He was perhaps eighteen and the muscles packed tightly beneath his lustrous black skin gave him a brooding strength. He came and stood outside the back door, his hands and lowered head performing the small, subtle rites of deference.

Mr. Watford's pleasure was full, for the gestures were those given only to a white man in his time. Yet the boy always nettled him. He sensed a natural arrogance like a pinpoint of light within his dark stare. The boy's stance exhumed a memory buried under the years. He remembered, staring at him, the time when he had worked as a yard boy for a white family, and had had to assume the same respectful pose while their flat, raw, Barbadian voices assailed him with orders. He remembered the muscles in his neck straining as he nodded deeply and a taste like alum on his tongue as he repeated the "Yes, please," as in a litany.

But, because of their whiteness and wealth, he had never dared hate them. Instead his rancor, like a boomerang, had rebounded, glancing past him to strike all the dark ones like himself, even his mother with her spindled arms and her stomach sagging with a child who was, invariably, dead at birth. He had been the only one of ten to live, the only one to escape. But he had never lost the sense of being pursued by the same dread presence which had claimed them. He had never lost the fear that if he lived too fully he would tire and death would quickly close the gap. His only defense had been a cautious life and work. He had been almost broken by work at the age of twenty when his parents died, leaving him enough money for the passage to America. Gladly had he fled the island. But nothing had mattered after his flight.

The boy's foot stirred the dust. He murmured, "Please, sir, Mr. Watford, Mr. Goodman at the shop send me to pick the coconuts."

Mr. Watford's head snapped up. A caustic word flared, but died as he noticed a political button pinned to the boy's patched shirt with "Vote for the Barbados People's Party" printed boldly on it, and below that the motto of the party: "The Old Order Shall Pass." At this ludicrous touch (for what could this boy, with his splayed and shigoed feet and blunted mind, understand about politics?) he became suddenly nervous, angry. The button and its motto seemed, somehow, directed at him. He said roughly, "Well, come then. You can't pick any coconuts standing there looking foolish!"—and he led the way to the grove.

The coconuts, he knew, would sell well at the booths in the center of the track, where the poor were penned in like cattle. As the heat thickened and the betting grew desperate, they would clamor: "Man, how you selling the water coconuts?" and hacking off the tops they would pour rum into the water within the hollow centers, then tilt the coconuts to their heads so that the rum-sweetened water skimmed their tongues and trickled bright down their dark chins. Mr. Watford had stood among them at the track as a young man, as poor as they were, but proud. And he had always found something unutterably graceful and free in their gestures, something which had roused contradictory feelings in him: admiration, but just as strong, impatience at their easy ways, and shame . . .

That night, as he sat in his white uniform reading, he heard Mr. Goodman's heavy step and went out and stood at the head of the stairs in a formal, proprietory pose. Mr. Goodman's face floated up into the light—the loose folds of flesh, the skin slick with sweat as if oiled, the eyes scribbled with veins and mottled, bold—as if each blemish there was a sin he proudly displayed or a scar which proved he had met life head-on. His body, unlike Mr. Watford's, was corpulent and, with the trousers caught up around his full crotch, openly concupiscent. He owned the one shop in the village which gave credit and a booth which sold coconuts at the race track, kept a wife and two outside women, drank a rum with each customer at his bar, regularly caned his fourteen children, who still followed him everywhere (even now they were waiting for him in the darkness beyond Mr. Watford's gate) and bet heavily at the races, and when he lost gave a loud hacking laugh which squeezed his body like a pain and left him gasping.

The laugh clutched him now as he flung his pendulous flesh into a chair and wheezed, "Watford, how? Man, I near lose house, shop, shirt and all at races today. I tell you, they got some horses from Trinidad in this meet that's making ours look like they running backwards. Be-Jese, I wouldn't bet on a Bajan horse tomorrow if Christ heself was to give me the tip. Those bitches might look good but they's nothing 'pon a track."

Mr. Watford, his back straight as the pillar he leaned against, his eyes unstained, his gaunt face planed by contempt, gave Mr. Goodman his cold, measured smile, thinking that the man would be dead soon, bloated with rice and rum—and somehow this made his own life more certain.

Sputtering with his amiable laughter, Mr. Goodman paid for the coconuts, but instead of leaving then as he usually did, he lingered, his eyes probing for a glimpse inside the house. Mr.

Watford waited, his head snapping warily; then, impatient, he started toward the door and Mr. Goodman said, "I tell you, your coconut trees bearing fast enough even for dwarfs. You's lucky, man."

Ordinarily Mr. Watford would have waved both the man and his remark aside, but repelled more than usual tonight by Mr. Goodman's gross form and immodest laugh, he said—glad of the cold edge his slight American accent gave the words —"What luck got to do with it? I does care the trees properly and they bear, that's all. Luck! People, especially this bunch around here, is always looking to luck when the only answer is a little brains and plenty of hard work. . . ." Suddenly remembering the boy that morning and the political button, he added in loud disgust, "Look that half-foolish boy you does send here to pick the coconuts. Instead of him learning a trade and going to England where he might find work he's walking about with a political button. He and all in politics now! But that's the way with these down in here. They'll do some of everything but work. They don't want work!" He gestured violently, almost dancing in anger. "They too busy spreeing."

The chair creaked as Mr. Goodman sketched a pained and gentle denial. "No, man," he said, "you wrong. Things is different to before. I mean to say, the young people nowadays is different to how we was. They not just sitting back and taking things no more. They not so frighten for the white people as we was. No man. Now take that said same boy, for an example. I don't say he don't like a spree, but he's serious, you see him there. He's a member of this new Barbados People's Party. He wants to see his own color running the government. He wants to be able to make a living right here in Barbados instead of going to any cold England. And he's right!" Mr. Goodman paused at a vehement pitch, then shrugged heavily. "What the young people must do, nuh? They got to look to something. . . ."

"Look to work!" And Mr. Watford thrust out a hand so that the horned knuckles caught the light.

"Yes, that's true—and it's up to we that got little something to give them work," Mr. Goodman said, and a sadness filtered among the dissipations in his eyes. "I mean to say we that got little something got to help out. In a manner of speaking, we's responsible . . ."

"Responsible!" The word circled Mr. Watford's head like a gnat and he wanted to reach up and haul it down, to squash it underfoot.

Mr. Goodman spread his hands; his breathing rumbled with a sigh. "Yes, in a manner of speaking. That's why, Watford man, you got to provide little work for some poor person down in here. Hire a servant at least! 'Cause I gon tell you something . . ." And he hitched forward his chair, his voice dropped to a wheeze. "People talking. Here you come back rich from big America and build a swell house and plant 'nough coconut trees and you still cleaning and cooking and thing like some woman? Man, it don't look good!" His face screwed in emphasis and he sat back. "Now there's this girl, the daughter of a friend that just dead, and she need work bad enough. But I wouldn't like to see she working for these white people 'cause you know how those men will take advantage of she. And she'd make a good servant, man. Quiet and quick so, and nothing a-tall to feed and she can sleep anywhere about the place. And she don't have no boys always around her either. . . ." Still talking, Mr. Goodman eased from his chair and reached the stairs with surprising agility. "You need a servant," he whispered, leaning close to Mr. Watford as he passed. "It don't look good, man. People talking. I gon send she."

Mr. Watford was overcome by nausea. Not only from Mr. Goodman's smell—a stench of salt fish, rum and sweat, but from an outrage which was like a sediment in his stomach. For a long time he stood there almost kecking from disgust, until his clock struck eight, reminding him of the sanctuary within—and suddenly his cold laugh dismissed Mr. Goodman and his proposal. Hurrying in, he locked the doors and windows against the night air and still laughing, he slept.

The next day, coming from the grove to prepare his noon meal, he saw her. She was standing in his driveway, her bare feet like strong dark roots amid the jagged stones, her face tilted toward the sun—and she might have been standing there always waiting for him. She seemed of the sun, of the earth. The folktale of creation might have been true with her: that along a river bank a god had scooped up the earth—rich and black and warmed by the sun—and molded her poised head with its tufted braids and then with a whimsical touch crowned it with a sober brown felt hat which should have been worn by some stout English matron in a London suburb, had sculptured the passionless face and drawn a screen of gossamer across her eyes to hide the void behind. Beneath her bodice her small breasts were smooth at the crest. Below her waist, her hips branched wide, the place prepared for its load of life. But it was the bold and sensual strength of her legs which completely unstrung Mr. Watford. He wanted to grab a hoe and drive her off.

"What it 'tis you want?" he called sharply.

"Mr. Goodman send me."

"Send you for what?" His voice was shrill in the glare.

She moved. Holding a caved-in valise and a pair

of white sandals, her head weaving slightly as
though she bore a pail of water there or a tray of
mangoes, she glided over the stones as if they
were smooth ground. Her bland expression did not
change, but her eyes, meeting his, held a vague
trust. Pausing a few feet away, she curtsied
deeply. "I's the new servant."

Only Mr. Watford's cold laugh saved him from
anger. As always it raised him to a height where
everything below appeared senseless and insignificant—especially his people, whom the girl
embodied. From this height, he could even be
charitable. And thinking suddenly of how she had
waited in the brutal sun since morning without
taking shelter under the nearby tamarind tree,
he said, not unkindly, "Well, girl, go back and
tell Mr. Goodman for me that I don't need no
servant."

"I can't go back."

"How you mean can't?" His head gave its
angry snap.

"I'll get lashes," she said simply. "My mother
say I must work the day and then if you don't
wish me, I can come back. But I's not to leave till
night falling, if not I get lashes."

He was shaken by her dispassion. So much so
that his head dropped from its disdaining angle
and his hands twitched with helplessness. Despite
anything he might say or do, her fear of the whip-
ping would keep her there until nightfall, the

valise and shoes in hand. He felt his day with its order and quiet rhythms threatened by her intrusion—and suddenly waving her off as if she were an evil visitation, he hurried into the kitchen to prepare his meal.

But he paused, confused, in front of the stove, knowing that he could not cook and leave her hungry at the door, nor could he cook and serve her as though he were the servant.

"You know anything about cooking?" he shouted finally.

"Yes, please."

They said nothing more. She entered the room with a firm step and an air almost of familiarity, placed her valise and shoes in a corner and went directly to the larder. For a time Mr. Watford stood by, his muscles flexing with anger and his eyes bounding ahead of her every move, until feeling foolish and frighteningly useless, he went out to feed his doves.

The meal was quickly done and as he ate he heard the dry slap of her feet behind him—a pleasant sound—and then silence. When he glanced back she was squatting in the doorway, the sunlight aslant the absurd hat and her face bent to a bowl she held in one palm. She ate slowly, thoughtfully, as if fixing the taste of each spoonful in her mind.

It was then that he decided to let her work the day and at nightfall to pay her a dollar and dismiss her. His decision held when he returned later from the grove and found tea awaiting him, and then through the supper she prepared. Afterward, dressed in his white uniform, he patiently waited out the day's end on the portico, his face setting into a grim mold. Then just as dusk etched the first dark line between the sea and sky, he took out a dollar and went downstairs.

She was not in the kitchen, but the table was set for his morning tea. Muttering at her persistence, he charged down the corridor, which ran the length of the basement, flinging open the doors to the damp, empty rooms on either side, and sending the lizards and the shadows long entrenched there scuttling to safety.

He found her in the small slanted room under the stoop, asleep on an old cot he kept there, her suitcase turned down beside the bed, and the shoes, dress and the ridiculous hat piled on top. A loose night shift muted the outline of her body and hid her legs, so that she appeared suddenly defenseless, innocent, with a child's trust in her curled hand and in her deep breathing. Standing in the doorway, with his own breathing snarled and his eyes averted, Mr. Watford felt like an intruder. She had claimed the room. Quivering with frustration, he slowly turned away, vowing that in the morning he would shove the dollar at her and lead her like a cow out of his house. . . .

Dawn brought rain and a hot wind which set

the leaves rattling and swiping at the air like distraught arms. Dressing in the dawn darkness, Mr.
Watford again armed himself with the dollar and,
with his shoulders at an uncompromising set,
plunged downstairs. He descended into the warm
smell of bakes and this smell, along with the
thought that she had been up before him, made
his hand knot with exasperation on the banister.
The knot tightened as he saw her, dust swirling at
her feet as she swept the corridor, her face bent
solemn to the task. Shutting her out with a lifted
hand, he shouted, "Don't bother sweeping. Here's
a dollar. G'long back."

The broom paused and although she did not
raise her head, he sensed her groping through the
shadowy maze of her mind toward his voice. Behind the dollar which he waved in her face, her
eyes slowly cleared. And, surprisingly, they held
no fear. Only anticipation and a tenuous trust. It
was as if she expected him to say something kind.

"G'long back!" His angry cry was a plea.

Like a small, starved flame, her trust and ex-
pectancy died and she said, almost with reproof,
"The rain falling."

To confirm this, the wind set the rain stinging
across the windows and he could say nothing, even
though the words sputtered at his lips. It was useless. There was nothing inside her to comprehend
that she was not wanted. His shoulders sagged under the weight of her ignorance, and with a futile

gesture he swung away, the dollar hanging from his hand like a small sword gone limp.

She became as fixed and familiar a part of the house as the stones—and as silent. He paid her five dollars a week, gave her Mondays off and in the evenings, after a time, even allowed her to sit in the alcove off the parlor, while he read with his back to her, taking no more notice of her than he did the moths on the lamp.

But once, after many silent evenings together, he detected a sound apart from the night murmurs of the sea and village and the metallic tuning of the steel band, a low, almost inhuman cry of loneliness which chilled him. Frightened, he turned to find her leaning hesitantly toward him, her eyes dark with urgency, and her face tight with bewilderment and a growing anger. He started, not understanding, and her arm lifted to stay him. Eagerly she bent closer. But as she uttered the low cry again, as her fingers described her wish to talk, he jerked around, afraid that she would be foolish enough to speak and that once she did they would be brought close. He would be forced then to acknowledge something about her which he refused to grant; above all, he would be called upon to share a little of himself. Quickly he returned to his newspaper, rustling it to settle the air, and after a time he felt her slowly, bitterly, return to her silence. . . .

Like sand poured in a careful measure from the

hand, the weeks flowed down to August and on the first Monday, August Bank holiday, Mr. Watford awoke to the sound of the excursion buses leaving the village for the annual outing, their backfire pelleting the dawn calm and the ancient motors protesting the overcrowding. Lying there, listening, he saw with disturbing clarity his mother dressed for an excursion—the white head tie wound above her dark face and her head poised like a dancer's under the heavy outing basket of food. That set of her head had haunted his years, reappearing in the girl as she walked toward him the first day. Aching with the memory, yet annoyed with himself for remembering, he went downstairs.

The girl had already left for the excursion, and although it was her day off, he felt vaguely betrayed by her eagerness to leave him. Somehow it suggested ingratitude. It was as if his doves were suddenly to refuse him their song or his trees their fruit, despite the care he gave them. Some vital part which shaped the simple mosaic of his life seemed suddenly missing. An alien silence curled like coal gas throughout the house. To escape it he remained in the grove all day and, upon his return to the house, dressed with more care than usual, putting on a fresh, starched uniform, and solemnly brushing his hair until it lay in a smooth bush above his brow. Leaning close to the mirror, but avoiding his eyes, he cleaned

the white rheum at their corners, and afterward
pried loose the dirt under his nails.

Unable to read his papers, he went out on the
portico to escape the unnatural silence in the
house, and stood with his hands clenched on the
balustrade and his taut body straining forward.
After a long wait he heard the buses return and
voices in gay shreds upon the wind. Slowly his
hands relaxed, as did his shoulders under the white
uniform; for the first time that day his breathing
was regular. She would soon come.

But she did not come and dusk bloomed into
night, with a fragrant heat and a full moon which
made the leaves glint as though touched with
frost. The steel band at the crossroads began the
lilting songs of sadness and seduction, and suddenly—like shades roused by the night and the
music—images of the girl flitted before Mr. Watford's eyes. He saw her lost amid the carousings
in the village, despoiled; he imagined someone
like Mr. Goodman clasping her lewdly or tumbling
her in the canebrake. His hand rose, trembling, to
rid the air of her; he tried to summon his cold
laugh. But, somehow, he could not dismiss her as
he had always done with everyone else. Instead, he
wanted to punish and protect her, to find and lead
her back to the house.

As he leaned there, trying not to give way to
the desire to go and find her, his fist striking the
balustrade to deny his longing, he saw them. The

girl first, with the moonlight like a silver patina
on her skin, then the boy whom Mr. Goodman sent
for the coconuts, whose easy strength and the
political button—"The Old Order Shall Pass"—
had always mocked and challenged Mr. Watford.
They were joined in a tender battle: the boy in
a sport shirt riotous with color was reaching for
the girl as he leaped and spun, weightless, to the
music, while she fended him off with a gesture
which was lovely in its promise of surrender. Her
protests were little scattered bursts: "But, man,
why you don't stop, nuh . . . ? But, you know,
you getting on like a real-real idiot. . . ."

Each time she chided him he leaped higher and
landed closer, until finally he eluded her arm and
caught her by the waist. Boldly he pressed a leg
between her tightly closed legs until they opened
under his pressure. Their bodies cleaved into one
whirling form and while he sang she laughed like
a wanton with her hat cocked over her ear. Dancing, the stones moiling underfoot, they claimed
the night. More than the night. The steel band
played for them alone. The trees were their frivolous companions, swaying as they swayed. The
moon rode the sky because of them.

Mr. Watford, hidden by a dense shadow, felt
the tendons which strung him together suddenly
go limp; above all, an obscure belief which, like
rare china, he had stored on a high shelf in his
mind began to tilt. He sensed the familiar specter

which hovered in the night reaching out to embrace him, just as the two in the yard were embracing. Utterly unstrung, incapable of either speech or action, he stumbled into the house, only to meet there an accusing silence from the clock, which had missed its eight o'clock winding, and his newspapers lying like ruined leaves over the floor.

He lay in bed in the white uniform, waiting for sleep to rescue him, his hands seeking the comforting sound of his doves. But sleep eluded him and instead of the doves, their throats tremulous with sound, his scarred hands filled with the shape of a woman he had once kept: her skin, which had been almost bruising in its softness; the buttocks and breasts spread under his hands to inspire both cruelty and tenderness. His hands closed to softly crush those forms, and the searing thrust of passion, which he had not felt for years, stabbed his dry groin. He imagined the two outside, their passion at a pitch by now, lying together behind the tamarind tree, or perhaps—and he sat up sharply —they had been bold enough to bring their lust into the house. Did he not smell their taint on the air? Restored suddenly, he rushed downstairs. As he reached the corridor, a thread of light beckoned him from her room and he dashed furiously toward it, rehearsing the angry words which would jar their bodies apart. He neared the door, glimpsed her through the small

opening, and his step faltered; the words collapsed.

She was seated alone on the cot, tenderly holding the absurd felt hat in her lap, one leg tucked
under her while the other trailed down. A white
sandal, its strap broken, dangled from the foot
and gently knocked the floor as she absently
swung her leg. Her dress was twisted around her
body—and pinned to the bodice, so that it gathered the cloth between her small breasts, was the
political button the boy always wore. She was
dreamily fingering it, her mouth shaped by a
gentle, ironic smile and her eyes strangely acute
and critical. What had transpired on the cot had
not only, it seemed, twisted the dress around her,
tumbled her hat and broken her sandal, but had
also defined her and brought the blurred forms of
life into focus for her. There was a woman's force
in her aspect now, a tragic knowing and accept-
ance in her bent head, a hint about her of Cas-
sandra watching the future wheel before her eyes.

Before those eyes which looked to another
world, Mr. Watford's anger and strength failed
him and he held to the wall for support. Unreasonably, he felt that he should assume some hushed
and reverent pose, to bow as she had the day she
had come. If he had known their names, he would
have pleaded forgiveness for the sins he had committed against her and the others all his life,
against himself. If he could have borne the

thought, he would have confessed that it had been love, terrible in its demand, which he had always fled. And that love had been the reason for his return. If he had been honest he would have whispered—his head bent and a hand shading his eyes —that unlike Mr. Goodman (whom he suddenly envied for his full life) and the boy with his political button (to whom he had lost the girl), he had not been willing to bear the weight of his own responsibility. . . . But all Mr. Watford could admit, clinging there to the wall, was, simply, that he wanted to live—and that the girl held life within her as surely as she held the hat in her hands. If he could prove himself better than the boy, he could win it. Only then, he dimly knew, would he shake off the pursuer which had given him no rest since birth. Hopefully, he staggered forward, his step cautious and contrite, his hands quivering along the wall.

She did not see or hear him as he pushed the door wider. And for some time he stood there, his shoulders hunched in humility, his skin stripped away to reveal each flaw, his whole self offered in one outstretched hand. Still unaware of him, she swung her leg, and the dangling shoe struck a derisive note. Then, just as he had turned away that evening in the parlor when she had uttered her low call, she turned away now, refusing him.

Mr. Watford's body went slack and then stiffened ominously. He knew that he would have to wrest from her the strength needed to sustain him. Slamming the door, he cried, his voice cracked and strangled, "What you and him was doing in here? Tell me! I'll not have you bringing nastiness round here. Tell me!"

She did not start. Perhaps she had been aware of him all along and had expected his outburst. Or perhaps his demented eye and the desperation rising from him like a musk filled her with pity instead of fear. Whatever, her benign smile held and her eyes remained abstracted until his hand reached out to fling her back on the cot. Then, frowning, she stood up, wobbling a little on the broken shoe and holding the political button as if it was a new power which would steady and protect her. With a cruel flick of her arm she struck aside his hand and, in a voice as cruel, halted him. "But you best move and don't come holding on to me, you nasty, pissy old man. That's all you is, despite yuh big house and fancy furnitures and yuh newspapers from America. You ain't people, Mr. Watford, you ain't people!" And with a look and a lift of her head which made her condemnation final, she placed the hat atop her braids, and turning aside picked up the valise which had always lain, packed, beside the cot—as if even on the first day she had known that this night would come and had been prepared against it. . . .

Mr. Watford did not see her leave, for a pain squeezed his heart dry and the driven blood was a bright, blinding cataract over his eyes. But his inner eye was suddenly clear. For the first time it gazed mutely upon the waste and pretense which had spanned his years. Flung there against the door by the girl's small blow, his body slowly crumpled under the weariness he had long denied. He sensed that dark but unsubstantial figure which roamed the nights searching for him wind him in its chill embrace. He struggled against it, his hands clutching the air with the spastic eloquence of a drowning man. He moaned—and the anguished sound reached beyond the room to fill the house. It escaped to the yard and his doves swelled their throats, moaning with him.

BROOKLYN

A summer wind, soaring

just before it died, blew the dusk and the first
scattered lights of downtown Brooklyn against
the shut windows of the classroom, but Professor
Max Berman—B.A., 1919, M.A., 1921, New
York; Docteur de l'Université, 1930, Paris—
alone in the room, did not bother to open the windows to the cooling wind. The heat and airlessness
of the room, the perspiration inching its way like
an ant around his starched collar were discom-
forts he enjoyed; they obscured his larger discomfort: the anxiety which chafed his heart and
tugged his left eyelid so that he seemed to be
winking, roguishly, behind his glasses.

To steady his eye and ease his heart, to fill the
time until his students arrived and his first class
in years began, he reached for his cigarettes. As
always he delayed lighting the cigarette so that
his need for it would be greater and, thus, the
relief and pleasure it would bring, fuller. For
some time he fondled it, his fingers shaping soft,
voluptuous gestures, his warped old man's hands
looking strangely abandoned on the bare desk and
limp as if the bones had been crushed, and so

white—except for the tobacco burn on the index
and third fingers—it seemed his blood no longer
traveled that far.

He lit the cigarette finally and as the smoke
swelled his lungs, his eyelid stilled and his lined
face lifted, the plume of white hair wafting above
his narrow brow; his body—short, blunt, the
shoulders slightly bent as if in deference to his
sixty-three years—settled back in the chair. Delicately Max Berman crossed his legs and, looking
down, examined his shoes for dust. (The shoes
were of a very soft, fawn-colored leather and
somewhat foppishly pointed at the toe. They had
been custom made in France and were his one last
indulgence. He wore them in memory of his first
wife, a French Jewess from Alsace-Lorraine
whom he had met in Paris while lingering over his
doctorate and married to avoid returning home.
She had been gay, mindless and very excitable—
but at night, she had also been capable of a profound stillness as she lay in bed waiting for him to
turn to her, and this had always awed and de-
lighted him. She had been a gift—and her death
in a car accident had been a judgment on him for
never having loved her, for never, indeed, having
even allowed her to matter.) Fastidiously Max
Berman unbuttoned his jacket and straightened
his vest, which had a stain two decades old on the
pocket. Through the smoke his veined eyes con-
templated other, more pleasurable scenes. With

his neatly shod foot swinging and his cigarette at a rakish tilt, he might have been an old *boulevardier* taking the sun and an absinthe before the afternoon's assignation.

A young face, the forehead shiny with earnestness, hung at the half-opened door. "Is this French Lit, fifty-four? Camus and Sartre?"

Max Berman winced at the rawness of the voice and the flat "a" in Sartre and said formally, "This is Modern French Literature, number fifty-four, yes, but there is some question as to whether we will take up Messieurs Camus and Sartre this session. They might prove hot work for a summer-evening course. We will probably do Gide and Mauriac, who are considerably more temperate. But come in nonetheless. . . ."

He was the gallant, half rising to bow her to a seat. He knew that she would select the one in the front row directly opposite his desk. At the bell her pen would quiver above her blank notebook, ready to commit his first word—indeed, the clearing of his throat—to paper, and her thin buttocks would begin sidling toward the edge of her chair.

His eyelid twitched with solicitude. He wished that he could have drawn the lids over her fitful eyes and pressed a cool hand to her forehead. She reminded him of what he had been several lifetimes ago: a boy with a pale, plump face and harried eyes, running from the occasional taunts at his yamilke along the shrill streets of Brownsville in Brooklyn, impeded by the heavy satchel of books which he always carried as proof of his scholarship. He had been proud of his brilliance at school and the Yeshiva, but at the same time he had been secretly troubled by it and resentful, for he could never believe that he had come by it naturally or that it belonged to him alone. Rather, it was like a heavy medal his father had hung around his neck—the chain bruising his flesh—and constantly exhorted him to wear proudly and use well.

The girl gave him an eager and ingratiating smile and he looked away. During his thirty years of teaching, a face similar to hers had crowded his vision whenever he had looked up from a desk. Perhaps it was fitting, he thought, and lighted another cigarette from the first, that she should be present as he tried again at life, unaware that behind his rimless glasses and within his ancient suit, he had been gutted.

He thought of those who had taken the last of his substance—and smiled tolerantly. "The boys of summer," he called them, his inquisitors, who had flailed him with a single question: "Are you now or have you ever been a member of the Communist party?" Max Berman had never taken their question seriously—perhaps because he had never taken his membership in the party seriously—and he had refused to answer. What had disturbed him, though, even when the investiga-

tion was over, was the feeling that he had really
been under investigation for some other offense
which did matter and of which he was guilty; that
behind their accusations and charges had lurked
another which had not been political but personal. For had he been disloyal to the government? His denial was a short, hawking laugh.
Simply, he had never ceased being religious.
When his father's God had become useless and
even a little embarrassing, he had sought others:
his work for a time, then the party. But he had
been middle-aged when he joined and his faith,
which had been so full as a boy, had grown thin.
He had come, by then, to distrust all pieties, so
that when the purges in Russia during the thirties
confirmed his distrust, he had withdrawn into a
modest cynicism.

But he had been made to answer for that error.
Ten years later his inquisitors had flushed him
out from the small community college in upstate
New York where he had taught his classes from
the same neat pack of notes each semester and had
led him bound by subpoena to New York and
bandied his name at the hearings until he had been
dismissed from his job.

He remembered looking back at the pyres of
burning autumn leaves on the campus his last day
and feeling that another lifetime had ended—for
he had always thought of his life as divided into
many small lives, each with its own beginning and

end. Like a hired mute, he had been present at each dying and kept the wake and wept professionally as the bier was lowered into the ground. Because of this feeling, he told himself that his final death would be anticlimactic.

After his dismissal he had continued living in the small house he had built near the college, alone except for an occasional visit from a colleague, idle but for some tutoring in French, content with the income he received from the property his parents had left him in Brooklyn—until the visits and tutoring had tapered off and a silence had begun to choke the house, like weeds springing up around a deserted place. He had begun to wonder then if he were still alive. He would wake at night from the recurrent dream of the hearings, where he was being accused of an unstated crime, to listen for his heart, his hand fumbling among the bedclothes to press the place. During the day he would pass repeatedly in front of the mirror with the pretext that he might have forgotten to shave that morning or that something had blown into his eye. Above all, he had begun to think of his inquisitors with affection and to long for the sound of their voices. They, at least, had assured him of being alive.

As if seeking them out, he had returned to Brooklyn and to the house in Brownsville where he had lived as a boy and had boldly applied for a teaching post without mentioning the investiga-

tion. He had finally been offered the class which
would begin in five minutes. It wasn't much: a
six-week course in the summer evening session of
a college without a rating, where classes were held
in a converted factory building, a college whose
campus took in the bargain department stores,
the five-and-dime emporiums and neon-spangled
movie houses of downtown Brooklyn.

Through the smoke from his cigarette, Max
Berman's eyes—a waning blue that never seemed
to focus on any one thing—drifted over the students who had gathered meanwhile. Imbuing them
with his own disinterest, he believed that even before the class began, most of them were longing for
its end and already anticipating the soft drinks
at the soda fountain downstairs and the synthetic
dramas at the nearby movie.

They made him sad. He would have liked to
lead them like a Pied Piper back to the safety of
their childhoods—all of them: the loud girl with
the formidable calves of an athlete who reminded
him, uncomfortably, of his second wife (a party
member who was always shouting political heresy
from some picket line and who had promptly di-
vorced him upon discovering his irreverence) ; the
two sallow-faced young men leaning out the window as if searching for the wind that had died ; the
slender young woman with crimped black hair
who sat very still and apart from the others, her
face turned toward the night sky as if to a friend.

Her loneliness interested him. He sensed its depth and his eye paused. He saw then that she was a Negro, a very pale mulatto with skin the color of clear, polished amber and a thin, mild face. She was somewhat older than the others in the room—a schoolteacher from the South, probably, who came north each summer to take courses toward a graduate degree. He felt a fleeting discomfort and irritation: discomfort at the thought that although he had been sinned against as a Jew he still shared in the sin against her and suffered from the same vague guilt, irritation that she recalled his own humiliations: the large ones, such as the fact that despite his brilliance he had been unable to get into a medical school as a young man because of the quota on Jews (not that he had wanted to be a doctor; that had been his father's wish) and had changed his studies from medicine to French; the small ones which had worn him thin: an eye widening imperceptibly as he gave his name, the savage glance which sought the Jewishness in his nose, his chin, in the set of his shoulders, the jokes snuffed into silence at his appearance. . . .

Tired suddenly, his eyelid pulsing, he turned and stared out the window at the gaudy constellation of neon lights. He longed for a drink, a quiet place and then sleep. And to bear him gently into sleep, to stay the terror which bound his heart then reminding him of those oleographs of Christ with the thorns binding his exposed heart—fat drops of blood from one so bloodless—to usher him into sleep, some pleasantly erotic image: a nude in a boudoir scattered with her frilled garments and warmed by her frivolous laugh, with the sun like a voyeur at the half-closed shutters. But this time instead of the usual Rubens nude with thighs like twin portals and a belly like a huge alabaster bowl into which he poured himself, he chose Gauguin's Aita Parari, her languorous form in the straight-back chair, her dark, sloping breasts, her eyes like the sun under shadow.

With the image still on his inner eye, he turned to the Negro girl and appraised her through a blind of cigarette smoke. She was still gazing out at the night sky and something about her fixed stare, her hands stiffly arranged in her lap, the nerve fluttering within the curve of her throat, betrayed a vein of tension within the rock of her calm. It was as if she had fled long ago to a remote region within herself, taking with her all that was most valuable and most vulnerable about herself.

She stirred finally, her slight breasts lifting beneath her flowered summer dress as she breathed deeply—and Max Berman thought again of Gauguin's girl with the dark, sloping breasts. What would this girl with the amber-colored skin be like on a couch in a sunlit room, nude in a straight-back chair? And as the question echoed along each nerve and stilled his breathing, it

seemed suddenly that life, which had scorned him
for so long, held out her hand again—but still a
little beyond his reach. Only the girl, he sensed,
could bring him close enough to touch it. She
alone was the bridge. So that even while he repeated to himself that he was being presumptu-
ous (for she would surely refuse him) and ridiculous (for even if she did not, what could he do—
his performance would be a mere scramble and
twitch), he vowed at the same time to have her.
The challenge eased the tightness around his heart
suddenly; it soothed the damaged muscle of his
eye and as the bell rang he rose and said briskly,
"Ladies and gentlemen, may I have your attention, please. My name is Max Berman. The course
is Modern French Literature, number fifty-four.
May I suggest that you check your program
cards to see whether you are in the right place at
the right time."

Her essay on Gide's *The Immoralist* lay on his
desk and the note from the administration informing him, first, that his past political activities had
been brought to their attention and then dismiss-
ing him at the end of the session weighed the inside pocket of his jacket. The two, her paper and
the note, were linked in his mind. Her paper reminded him that the vow he had taken was still an
empty one, for the term was half over and he had
never once spoken to her (as if she understood his

intention she was always late and disappeared as
soon as the closing bell rang, leaving him trapped
in a clamorous circle of students around his desk),
while the note which wrecked his small attempt
to start anew suddenly made that vow more urgent. It gave him the edge of desperation he
needed to act finally. So that as soon as the bell
rang, he returned all the papers but hers, announced that all questions would have to wait until their next meeting and, waving off the students
from his desk, called above their protests, "Miss
Williams, if you have a moment, I'd like to speak
with you briefly about your paper."

She approached his desk like a child who has
been cautioned not to talk to strangers, her fingers
touching the backs of the chair as if for support,
her gaze following the departing students as
though she longed to accompany them.

Her slight apprehensiveness pleased him. It
suggested a submissiveness which gave him, as he
rose uncertainly, a feeling of certainty and command. Her hesitancy was somehow in keeping with
the color of her skin. She seemed to bring not only
herself but the host of black women whose bodies
had been despoiled to make her. He would not
only possess her but them also, he thought (not
really thought, for he scarcely allowed these
thoughts to form before he snuffed them out).
Through their collective suffering, which she contained, his own personal suffering would be eased;

he would be pardoned for whatever sin it was he had committed against life.

"I hope you weren't unduly alarmed when I didn't return your paper along with the others," he said, and had to look up as she reached the desk. She was taller close up and her eyes, which he had thought were black, were a strong, flecked brown with very small pupils which seemed to shrink now from the sight of him. "But I found it so interesting I wanted to give it to you privately."

"I didn't know what to think," she said, and her voice—he heard it for the first time for she never recited or answered in class—was low, cautious, Southern.

"It was, to say the least, refreshing. It not only showed some original and mature thinking on your part, but it also proved that you've been listening in class—and after twenty-five years and more of teaching it's encouraging to find that some students do listen. If you have a little time I'd like to tell you, more specifically, what I liked about it. . . ."

Talking easily, reassuring her with his professional tone and a deft gesture with his cigarette, he led her from the room as the next class filed in, his hand cupped at her elbow but not touching it, his manner urbane, courtly, kind. They paused on the landing at the end of the long corridor with the stairs piled in steel tiers above and plunging below them. An intimate silence swept up the stairwell in a warm gust and Max Berman said, "I'm curious. Why did you choose *The Immoralist?*"

She started suspiciously, afraid, it seemed, that her answer might expose and endanger the self she guarded so closely within.

"Well," she said finally, her glance reaching down the stairs to the door marked EXIT at the bottom, "when you said we could use anything by Gide I decided on *The Immoralist,* since it was the first book I read in the original French when I was in undergraduate school. I didn't understand it then because my French was so weak, I guess, but I always thought about it afterward for some odd reason. I was shocked by what I did understand, of course, but something else about it appealed to me, so when you made the assignment I thought I'd try reading it again. I understood it a little better this time. At least I think so. . . ."

"Your paper proves you did."

She smiled absently, intent on some other thought. Then she said cautiously, but with unexpected force, "You see, to me, the book seems to say that the only way you begin to know what you are and how much you are capable of is by daring to try something, by doing something which tests you. . . ."

"Something bold," he said.

"Yes."

"Even sinful."

She paused, questioning this, and then said reluctantly, "Yes, perhaps even sinful."

"The salutary effects of sin, you might say." He gave the little bow.

But she had not heard this; her mind had already leaped ahead. "The only trouble, at least with the character in Gide's book, is that what he finds out about himself is so terrible. He is so unhappy. . . ."

"But at least he knows, poor sinner." And his playful tone went unnoticed.

"Yes," she said with the same startling forcefulness. "And another thing, in finding out what he is, he destroys his wife. It was as if she had to die in order for him to live and know himself. Perhaps in order for a person to live and know himself somebody else must die. Maybe there's always a balancing out. . . . In a way"—and he had to lean close now to hear her—"I believe this."

Max Berman edged back as he glimpsed something move within her abstracted gaze. It was like a strong and restless seed that had taken root in the darkness there and was straining now toward the light. He had not expected so subtle and complex a force beneath her mild exterior and he found it disturbing and dangerous, but fascinating.

"Well, it's a most interesting interpretation,"

he said. "I don't know if M. Gide would have agreed, but then he's not around to give his opinion. Tell me, where did you do your under-graduate work?"

"At Howard University."

"And you majored in French?"

"Yes."

"Why, if I may ask?" he said gently.

"Well, my mother was from New Orleans and could still speak a little Creole and I got in-terested in learning how to speak French through her, I guess. I teach it now at a junior high school in Richmond. Only the beginner courses because I don't have my master's. You know, *je vais, tu vas, il va* and *Frère Jacques*. It's not very in-spiring."

"You should do something about that then, my dear Miss Williams. Perhaps it's time for you, like our friend in Gide, to try something new and bold."

"I know," she said, and her pale hand sketched a vague, despairing gesture. "I thought maybe if I got my master's . . . that's why I decided to come north this summer and start taking some courses. . . ."

Max Berman quickly lighted a cigarette to still the flurry inside him, for the moment he had been awaiting had come. He flicked her paper, which he still held. "Well, you've got the makings of a master's thesis right here. If you like I will suggest some ways for you to expand it sometime. A few pointers from an old pro might help."

He had to turn from her astonished and grateful smile—it was like a child's. He said carefully, "The only problem will be to find a place where we can talk quietly. Regrettably, I don't rate an office. . . ."

"Perhaps we could use one of the empty classrooms," she said.

"That would be much too dismal a setting for a pleasant discussion."

He watched the disappointment wilt her smile and when he spoke he made certain that the same disappointment weighed his voice. "Another difficulty is that the term's half over, which gives us little or no time. But let's not give up. Perhaps we can arrange to meet and talk over a weekend. The only hitch there is that I spend weekends at my place in the country. Of course you're perfectly welcome to come up there. It's only about seventy miles from New York, in the heart of what's very appropriately called the Borsch Circuit, even though, thank God, my place is a good distance away from the borsch. That is, it's very quiet and there's never anybody around except with my permission."

She did not move, yet she seemed to start; she made no sound, yet he thought he heard a bewildered cry. And then she did a strange thing, standing there with the breath sucked into the hollow of her throat and her smile, that had opened to him with such trust, dying—her eyes, her hands faltering up begged him to declare himself.

"There's a lake near the house," he said, "so that when you get tired of talking—or better, listening to me talk—you can take a swim, if you like. I would very much enjoy that sight." And as the nerve tugged at his eyelid, he seemed to wink behind his rimless glasses.

Her sudden, blind step back was like a man groping his way through a strange room in the dark, and instinctively Max Berman reached out to break her fall. Her arms, bare to the shoulder because of the heat (he knew the feel of her skin without even touching it—it would be like a rich, fine-textured cloth which would soothe and hide him in its amber warmth), struck out once to drive him off and then fell limp at her side, and her eyes became vivid and convulsive in her numbed face. She strained toward the stairs and the exit door at the bottom, but she could not move. Nor could she speak. She did not even cry. Her eyes remained dry and dull with disbelief. Only her shoulders trembled as though she was silently weeping inside.

It was as though she had never learned the forms and expressions of anger. The outrage of a lifetime, of her history, was trapped inside her. And she stared at Max Berman with this mute, paralyzing rage. Not really at him but to his side,

as if she caught sight of others behind him. And
remembering how he had imagined a column of
dark women trailing her to his desk, he sensed that
she glimpsed a legion of old men with sere flesh
and lonely eyes flanking him: "old lechers with a
love on every wind . . ."

"I'm sorry, Miss Williams," he said, and would
have welcomed her insults, for he would have been
able, at least, to distill from them some passion
and a kind of intimacy. It would have been, in a
way, like touching her. "It was only that you are
a very attractive young woman and although I'm
no longer young"—and he gave the tragic little
laugh which sought to dismiss that fact—"I can
still appreciate and even desire an attractive
woman. But I was wrong. . . ." His self-disgust,
overwhelming him finally, choked off his voice.
"And so very crude. Forgive me. I can offer no
excuse for my behavior other than my approaching senility."

He could not even manage the little marionette
bow this time. Quickly he shoved the paper on
Gide into her lifeless hand, but it fell, the pages
separating, and as he hurried past her downstairs
and out the door, he heard the pages scattering
like dead leaves on the steps.

She remained away until the night of the final
examination, which was also the last meeting of
the class. By that time Max Berman, believing

that she would not return, had almost succeeded in forgetting her. He was no longer even certain of how she looked, for her face had been absorbed into the single, blurred, featureless face of all the women who had ever refused him. So that she startled him as much as a stranger would have when he entered the room that night and found her alone amid a maze of empty chairs, her face turned toward the window as on the first night and her hands serene in her lap. She turned at his footstep and it was as if she had also forgotten all that had passed between them. She waited until he said, "I'm glad you decided to take the examination. I'm sure you won't have any difficulty with it"; then she gave him a nod that was somehow reminiscent of his little bow and turned again to the window.

He was relieved yet puzzled by her composure. It was as if during her three-week absence she had waged and won a decisive contest with herself and was ready now to act. He was wary suddenly and all during the examination he tried to discover what lay behind her strange calm, studying her bent head amid the shifting heads of the other students, her slim hand guiding the pen across the page, her legs—the long bone visible, it seemed, beneath the flesh. Desire flared and quickly died.

"Excuse me, Professor Berman, will you take up Camus and Sartre next semester, maybe?" The girl who sat in front of his desk was standing over him with her earnest smile and finished examination folder.

"That might prove somewhat difficult, since I won't be here."

"No more?"

"No."

"I mean, not even next summer?"

"I doubt it."

"Gee, I'm sorry. I mean, I enjoyed the course and everything."

He bowed his thanks and held his head down until she left. Her compliment, so piteous somehow, brought on the despair he had forced to the dim rear of his mind. He could no longer flee the thought of the exile awaiting him when the class tonight ended. He could either remain in the house in Brooklyn, where the memory of his father's face above the radiance of the Sabbath candles haunted him from the shadows, reminding him of the certainty he had lost and never found again, where the mirrors in his father's room were still shrouded with sheets, as on the day he lay dying and moaning into his beard that his only son was a bad Jew; or he could return to the house in the country, to the silence shrill with loneliness.

The cigarette he was smoking burned his fingers, rousing him, and he saw over the pile of examination folders on his desk that the room was empty except for the Negro girl. She had finished—her pen lay aslant the closed folder on her desk—but she had remained in her seat and she was smiling across the room at him—a set, artificial smile that was both cold and threatening. It utterly denuded him and he was wildly angry suddenly that she had seen him give way to despair; he wanted to remind her (he could not stay the thought; it attacked him like an assailant from a dark turn in his mind) that she was only black after all. . . . His head dropped and he almost wept with shame.

The girl stiffened as if she had seen the thought and then the tiny muscles around her mouth quickly arranged the bland smile. She came up to his desk, placed her folder on top of the others and said pleasantly, her eyes like dark, shattered glass that spared Max Berman his reflection, "I've changed my mind. I think I'd like to spend a day at your place in the country if your invitation still holds."

He thought of refusing her, for her voice held neither promise nor passion, but he could not. Her presence, even if it was only for a day, would make his return easier. And there was still the possibility of passion despite her cold manner and the deliberate smile. He thought of how long it had been since he had had someone, of how badly he needed the sleep which followed love and of awakening certain, for the first time in years, of his existence.

"Of course the invitation still holds. I'm driving up tonight."

"I won't be able to come until Sunday," she said firmly. "Is there a train then?"

"Yes, in the morning," he said, and gave her the schedule.

"You'll meet me at the station?"

"Of course. You can't miss my car. It's a very shabby but venerable Chevy."

She smiled stiffly and left, her heels awakening the silence of the empty corridor, the sound reaching back to tap like a warning finger on Max Berman's temple.

The pale sunlight slanting through the windshield lay like a cat on his knees, and the motor of his old Chevy, turning softly under him could have been the humming of its heart. A little distance from the car a log-cabin station house—the logs blackened by the seasons—stood alone against the hills, and the hills, in turn, lifted softly, still green although the summer was ending, into the vague autumn sky.

The morning mist and pale sun, the green that was still somehow new, made it seem that the season was stirring into life even as it died, and this contradiction pained Max Berman at the same time that it pleased him. For it was his own contradiction after all: his desires which remained those of a young man even as he was dying.

He had been parked for some time in the deserted station, yet his hands were still tensed on the steering wheel and his foot hovered near the accelerator. As soon as he had arrived in the station he had wanted to leave. But like the girl that night on the landing, he was too stiff with tension to move. He could only wait, his eyelid twitching with foreboding, regret, curiosity and hope.

Finally and with no warning the train charged through the fiery green, setting off a tremor underground. Max Berman imagined the girl seated at a window in the train, her hands arranged quietly in her lap and her gaze scanning the hills that were so familiar to him, and yet he could not believe that she was really there. Perhaps her plan had been to disappoint him. She might be in New York or on her way back to Richmond now, laughing at the trick she had played on him. He was convinced of this suddenly, so that even when he saw her walking toward him through the blown steam from under the train, he told himself that she was a mirage created by the steam. Only when she sat beside him in the car, bringing with her, it seemed, an essence she had distilled from the morning air and rubbed into her skin, was he certain of her reality.

"I brought my bathing suit but it's much too cold to swim," she said and gave him the deliberate smile.

He did not see it; he only heard her voice, its

warm Southern lilt in the chill, its intimacy in the closed car—and an excitement swept him, cold first and then hot, as if the sun had burst in his blood.

"It's the morning air," he said. "By noon it should be like summer again."

"Is that a promise?"

"Yes."

By noon the cold morning mist had lifted above the hills and below, in the lake valley, the sunlight was a sheer gold net spread out on the grass as if to dry, draped on the trees and flung, glinting, over the lake. Max Berman felt it brush his shoulders gently as he sat by the lake waiting for the girl, who had gone up to the house to change into her swimsuit.

He had spent the morning showing her the fields and small wood near his house. During the long walk he had been careful to keep a little apart from her. He would extend a hand as they climbed a rise or when she stepped uncertainly over a rock, but he would not really touch her. He was afraid that at his touch, no matter how slight and casual, her scream would spiral into the morning calm, or worse, his touch would unleash the threatening thing he sensed behind her even smile.

He had talked of her paper and she had listened politely and occasionally even asked a question or made a comment. But all the while detached, distant, drawn within herself as she had been that

first night in the classroom. And then halfway
down a slope she had paused and, pointing to the
canvas tops of her white sneakers, which had become wet and dark from the dew secreted in the
grass, she had laughed. The sound, coming so
abruptly in the midst of her tense quiet, joined
her, it seemed, to the wood and wide fields, to the
hills; she shared their simplicity and held within
her the same strong current of life. Max Berman
had felt privileged suddenly, and humble. He had
stopped questioning her smile. He had told himself then that it would not matter even if she
stopped and picking up a rock bludgeoned him
from behind.

"There's a lake near my home, but it's not like
this," the girl said, coming up behind him. "Yours
is so dark and serious-looking."

He nodded and followed her gaze out to the lake,
where the ripples were long, smooth welts raised
by the wind, and across to the other bank, where
a group of birches stepped delicately down to the
lake and bending over touched the water with
their branches as if testing it before they plunged.

The girl came and stood beside him now—and
she was like a pale-gold naiad, the spirit of the
lake, her eyes reflecting its somber autumnal tone
and her body as supple as the birches. She walked
slowly into the water, unaware, it seemed, of the
sudden passion in his gaze, or perhaps uncaring;
and as she walked she held out her arms in what

seemed a gesture of invocation (and Max Berman remembered his father with the fringed shawl draped on his outstretched arms as he invoked their God each Sabbath with the same gesture); her head was bent as if she listened for a voice beneath the water's murmurous surface. When the ground gave way she still seemed to be walking and listening, her arms outstretched. The water reached her waist, her small breasts, her shoulders. She lifted her head once, breathed deeply and disappeared.

She stayed down for a long time and when her white cap finally broke the water some distance out, Max Berman felt strangely stranded and deprived. He understood suddenly the profound cleavage between them and the absurdity of his hope. The water between them became the years which separated them. Her white cap was the sign of her purity, while the silt darkening the lake was the flotsam of his failures. Above all, their color—her arms a pale, flashing gold in the sunlit water and his bled white and flaccid with the veins like angry blue penciling—marked the final barrier.

He was sad as they climbed toward the house late that afternoon and troubled. A crow cawed derisively in the bracken, heralding the dusk which would not only end their strange day but would also, he felt, unveil her smile, so that he would learn the reason for her coming. And because he was sad, he said wryly, "I think I should tell you that you've been spending the day with something of an outcast."

"Oh," she said and waited.

He told her of the dismissal, punctuating his words with the little hoarse, deprecating laugh and waving aside the pain with his cigarette. She listened, polite but neutral, and because she remained unmoved, he wanted to confess all the more. So that during dinner and afterward when they sat outside on the porch, he told her of the investigation.

"It was very funny once you saw it from the proper perspective, which I did, of course," he said. "I mean here they were accusing me of crimes I couldn't remember committing and asking me for the names of people with whom I had never associated. It was pure farce. But I made a mistake. I should have done something dramatic or something just as farcical. Bared my breast in the public market place or written a tome on my apostasy, naming names. It would have been a far different story then. Instead of my present ignominy I would have been offered a chairmanship at Yale. . . . No? Well, Brandeis then. I would have been draped in honorary degrees. . . ."

"Well, why didn't you confess?" she said impatiently.

"I've often asked myself the same interesting

question, but I haven't come up with a satisfactory answer yet. I suspect, though, that I said nothing because none of it really mattered that much."

"What did matter?" she asked sharply.

He sat back, waiting for the witty answer, but none came, because just then the frame upon which his organs were strung seemed to snap and he felt his heart, his lungs, his vital parts fall in a heap within him. Her question had dealt the severing blow, for it was the same question he understood suddenly that the vague forms in his dream asked repeatedly. It had been the plaintive undercurrent to his father's dying moan, the real accusation behind the charges of his inquisitors at the hearing.

For what had mattered? He gazed through his sudden shock at the night squatting on the porch steps, at the hills asleep like gentle beasts in the darkness, at the black screen of the sky where the events of his life passed in a mute, accusing review—and he saw nothing there to which he had given himself or in which he had truly believed since the belief and dedication of his boyhood.

"Did you hear my question?" she asked, and he was glad that he sat within the shadows clinging to the porch screen and could not be seen.

"Yes, I did," he said faintly, and his eyelid twitched. "But I'm afraid it's another one of those

I can't answer satisfactorily." And then he struggled for the old flippancy. "You make an excellent examiner, you know. Far better than my inquisitors."

"What will you do now?" Her voice and cold smile did not spare him.

He shrugged and the motion, a slow, eloquent lifting of the shoulders, brought with it suddenly the weight and memory of his boyhood. It was the familiar gesture of the women hawkers in Belmont Market, of the men standing outside the temple on Saturday mornings, each of them reflecting his image of God in their forbidding black coats and with the black, tumbling beards in which he had always imagined he could hide as in a forest. All this had mattered, he called loudly to himself, and said aloud to the girl, "Let me see if I can answer this one at least. What *will* I do?" He paused and swung his leg so that his foot in the fastidious French shoe caught the light from the house. "Grow flowers and write my memoirs. How's that? That would be the proper way for a gentleman and scholar to retire. Or hire one of those hefty housekeepers who will bully me and when I die in my sleep draw the sheet over my face and call my lawyer. That's somewhat European, but how's that?"

When she said nothing for a long time, he added soberly, "But that's not a fair question for me any more. I leave all such considerations to the young. To you, for that matter. What will you do, my dear Miss Williams?"

It was as if she had been expecting the question and had been readying her answer all the time that he had been talking. She leaned forward eagerly and with her face and part of her body fully in the light, she said, "I will do something. I don't know what yet, but something."

Max Berman started back a little. The answer was so unlike her vague, resigned "I know" on the landing that night when he had admonished her to try something new.

He edged back into the darkness and she leaned further into the light, her eyes overwhelming her face and her mouth set in a thin, determined line. "I will do something," she said, bearing down on each word, "because for the first time in my life I feel almost brave."

He glimpsed this new bravery behind her hard gaze and sensed something vital and purposeful, precious, which she had found and guarded like a prize within her center. He wanted it. He would have liked to snatch it and run like a thief. He no longer desired her but it, and starting forward with a sudden envious cry, he caught her arm and drew her close, seeking it.

But he could not get to it. Although she did not pull away her arm, although she made no protest as his face wavered close to hers, he did not really

touch her. She held herself and her prize out of his
desperate reach and her smile was a knife she
pressed to his throat. He saw himself for what he
was in her clear, cold gaze: an old man with skin
the color and texture of dough that had been
kneaded by the years into tragic folds, with faded
eyes adrift behind a pair of rimless glasses and
the roughened flesh at his throat like a bird's wat-
tles. And as the disgust which he read in her eyes
swept him, his hand dropped from her arm. He
started to murmur, "Forgive me . . ." when suddenly she caught hold of his wrist, pulling him
close again, and he felt the strength which had
borne her swiftly through the water earlier hold
him now as she said quietly and without passion,
"And do you know why, Dr. Berman, I feel almost brave today? Because ever since I can remember my parents were always telling me, 'Stay
away from white folks. Just leave them alone. You
mind your business and they'll mind theirs. Don't
go near them.' And they made sure I didn't. My
father, who was the principal of a colored grade
school in Richmond, used to drive me to and from
school every day. When I needed something from
downtown my mother would take me and if the
white saleslady asked me anything she would
answer. . . .

"And my parents were also always telling me,
'Stay away from niggers,' and that meant anybody
darker than we were." She held out her arm in the

light and Max Berman saw the skin almost as white as his but for the subtle amber shading. Staring at the arm she said tragically, "I was so confused I never really went near anybody. Even when I went away to college I kept to myself. I didn't marry the man I wanted to because he was dark and I knew my parents would disapprove. . . ." She paused, her wistful gaze searching the darkness for the face of the man she had refused, it seemed, and not finding it she went on sadly, "So after graduation I returned home and started teaching and I was just as confused and frightened and ashamed as always. When my parents died I went on the same way. And I would have gone on like that the rest of my life if it hadn't been for you, Dr. Berman"—and the sarcasm leaped behind her cold smile. "In a way you did me a favor. You let me know how you—and most of the people like you—see me."

"My dear Miss Williams, I assure you I was not attracted to you because you were colored. . . ." And he broke off, remembering just how acutely aware of her color he had been.

"I'm not interested in your reasons!" she said brutally. "What matters is what it meant to me. I thought about this these last three weeks and about my parents—how wrong they had been, how frightened, and the terrible thing they had done to me . . . And I wasn't confused any longer." Her head lifted, tremulous with her new assurance.

"I can do something now! I can begin," she said
with her head poised. "Look how I came all the
way up here to tell you this to your face. Because
how could you harm me? You're so old you're like
a cup I could break in my hand." And her hand
tightened on his wrist, wrenching the last of his
frail life from him, it seemed. Through the quick
pain he remembered her saying on the landing
that night: "Maybe in order for a person to live
someone else must die" and her quiet "I believe
this" then. Now her sudden laugh, an infinitely
cruel sound in the warm night, confirmed her belief.

Suddenly she was the one who seemed old, indeed ageless. Her touch became mortal and Max
Berman saw the darkness that would end his life
gathered in her eyes. But even as he sprang back,
jerking his arm away, a part of him rushed forward to embrace that darkness, and his cry,
wounding the night, held both ecstasy and terror.

"That's all I came for," she said, rising. "You
can drive me to the station now."

They drove to the station in silence. Then, just
as the girl started from the car, she turned with
an ironic, pitiless smile and said, "You know, it's
been a nice day, all things considered. It really
turned summer again as you said it would. And
even though your lake isn't anything like the one
near my home, it's almost as nice."

Max Berman bowed to her for the last time, accepting with that gesture his responsibility for her rage, which went deeper than his, and for her anger, which would spur her finally to live. And not only for her, but for all those at last whom he had wronged through his indifference: his father lying in the room of shrouded mirrors, the wives he had never loved, his work which he had never believed in enough and, lastly (even though he knew it was too late and he would not be spared), himself.

Too weary to move, he watched the girl cross to the train which would bear her south, her head lifted as though she carried life as lightly there as if it were a hat made of tulle. When the train departed his numbed eyes followed it until its rear light was like a single firefly in the immense night or the last flickering of his life. Then he drove back through the darkness.

BRITISH GUIANA

"Bowl him out, man!

Bowl him out!"

The week-long, unseasonable rain had only just ended but the village boys had already planted their wicket (three parallel sticks with a flat stone teetering on top) like a sign of conquest in the muddy road and were intent at a cricket game, their shouts of "Bowl him out" defying the ruin and desolation of the drenched land and their own hunger, their bodies—so Gerald Motley thought as he saw them through the last of the rain stippling his windshield—mere stick figures draped in dun-colored rags. At the sound of his horn they scattered, the rags flapping like wings, and stood on either side of the road with the mud sucking between their bare toes and their eyes white with worry in their dark faces as the battered Jaguar sedan bore recklessly down on their abandoned wicket. But as it swerved past in a spume of mud and Gerald Motley waved and shouted, "Get him on the outside next time, boys," their shrill, deferent cry of "Morning, Mr. Motts" pierced the morning pall and their laughter promised that the sun would soon heave into sight above the scudding clouds.

Oddly, their familiar shouts this morning reminded him of sounds he sometimes heard during sleep. At the beginning of sleep when he hovered —feeling small despite his bulk, and somehow vulnerable—between consciousness and a welling dream. As these two wrestled to win him—consciousness calling him back for another rum at Ling's, sleep beckoning him with the fabulous form of some dream—he would struggle on the bed and call for his old nurse, who had died decades ago. Now the boys' cries seemed to call him away from a dangerous dream he was pursuing unawares, to urge him toward life again, and as their warning was snatched by a damp gust, Gerald Motley became suddenly wary of the day.

This small caution sounding faintly beneath the irreverent laugh which summed up all that Gerald Motley felt about himself woke him fully and even sobered him, so that last night's drinking was no more now than a taste like that of his own decay in his mouth and a dull gnawing in his stomach as an old ulcer stirred vaguely into life. But the slight pain would cease, the taste would vanish once he had had his first drink for the morning.

To assure himself of this, he glanced at his reflection in the rear-view mirror and, as always, smilingly lifted his Panama hat in apology. For the reflection could have been a stranger's face, someone with whom he had collided on a busy street in Georgetown, some Englishman, perhaps, who had remained in B.G.—British Guiana—too long and whose aging face revealed the damage done by the rum, the pitiless Guianese sun and his own lost purpose. The reflection had nothing to do with the only image Gerald Motley held of himself, the only one he permitted to consciousness: this was of a young man in a photograph taken forty years ago on the eve of his return to B.G. from school in England.

He had been handsome then, with a taut athlete's body astride a pair of muscular legs, powerful arms which gauged the fullness of his young strength as they hung at his side, a fine head set at an assured angle and a gaze which reached beyond the frame of the photograph to probe the future with confidence.

He could have been white then (and he had often been taken for an Italian or Spaniard in England), for early in his long complex history a British Army officer sent out to B.G. had bequeathed him the thin features, the fair skin and hair; or black, since the slave woman the officer had used once and forgotten had passed her dark hand lightly over his paleness and claimed him with a full expressive mouth; or East Indian, for some Hindu brought to the colony along with the Chinese when the slave trade was over had added a marked passion and tension to his thin nose and touched his eyes with an abstract and mystical fire.

He was all these strains, yet no one singly, and because of this he was called in B.G. creole or colored—*high-colored*, since his family had once been modestly wealthy and very proud. But Gerald Motley had dissipated that wealth and he had even begun to betray that pride, for occasionally now when he had had enough to drink so that his vision of himself was clear and his voice so slurred he could not be understood, he would call out in a bar or at a crowded party, "The name, gentlemen? Gerald Ramsdeen Motley. My title, sirs? B.S.W.C.; Bastard Spawned of the World's Commingling!"—the words raveling on the sharp edge of his laughter.

This sense of being many things and yet none, this confusion, had set the mold of his life. He wanted to be, to know, everything. So that, as a student in England, he had read law at the Inns of Court for a time, begun medicine at Edinburgh, studied economics at the London School for a short period and the classics at Oxford. His stay at each school had been brilliant but brief, and at thirty-four he had left England well-educated but without a career.

Once home, he had again taken his place among the high-coloreds of Georgetown, enjoying his privileged life in the large colonial house on Dodds Road (and he still lived there, alone, the last of his line), sharing his class's indifference to the colony's troubles, moving through the round of jobs his father and uncles had secured for him before they died and, at the appropriate time, he had married the fair-complexioned daughter of a highly respected Georgetown family and had had a child.

But even then he had managed to contradict all this by frequenting the notorious sailor bars along Water Street to drink rum and shout politics with the stevedores there—he had even once, they say, attempted to lead them in a strike against Orly Shipping Ltd. And, worse, a year after his marriage, he had met Sybil Jeffries, a part-Chinese Negro girl from a village outside Georgetown and begun the long, bold affair that was to send his wife and child to America (where they passed for white and forgot him) and, inadvertently, make him a successful man.

Gerald Motley pressed the accelerator (he might have been fleeing the thought of Sybil Jeffries) and the big car seemed to pause and assess his mood and then surged forward like an animal gathering speed as it ran. The land on both sides of the narrow road stretched like a vast, empty stage waiting for the props and players to visit it with life, and as Gerald Motley entered a Hindu village, the props appeared—the sun-bleached wooden houses raised on stilts above the flooded ground, the frayed prayer flags on tall poles outside each house, the mosques angled toward Mecca and the swarms of Hindu children digging for shrimp in the mud of the drainage trenches which lined the road, while their mothers swathed in saris squatted under the gnarled, leafless forms of the saman trees.

A small rice field ended the village. It had been ruined by the unseasonable rain and the Hindu family who owned it stood in the flooded field surveying their loss, small bowed shapes beneath an indifferent sky. The rice field yielded to an interminable wall of sugar cane and, as he sped by, the black men cutting the cane paused and held their machetes at a quivering height for a moment, and he waved back. These were the forms and rituals of the land and each morning on his long, sobering drives into the country outside Georgetown Gerald Motley sought their meanings. . . .

He had reached the sea wall which guarded the land from a brown and sluggish sea when the sun which the boys' laughter had promised rose like a tarnished coin above the immense bush surrounding Georgetown. It was as if the sun had come from out of the bush, as if it had been spawned within its dark vitals—so Gerald Motley thought as he saw it rise each morning and remembered the one time he had been in the bush. It had been almost thirty years ago, just after he had been offered his present position as program director for B.G. Broadcasting and just before he had decided to accept the job. Thinking back now, he could no longer recall what Cyril Orly, who had not only owned the broadcasting station but the large sugar estates in B.G., the big shops in Georgetown and most of the colony's shipping interests, had said. It had been something like:

"I hear you're bright, Motley, and something of an organizer down on Water Street at nights. If you could perhaps transfer those talents to our camp, you might prove just the sort of chap we need to get the new broadcasting station under way. We'd send you to England for a few courses with the B.B.C. Of course, I don't have to tell you what this would mean. You'd be the first colored man in the West Indies to hold this high a position in broadcasting. . . ."

But he remembered clearly Cyril Orly's face, although he had been dead many years now and his son, Frank, ruled. Veins had fingered the white parchment skin. The eyes had still been shrewd beneath their thick rheum. Gerald Motley remembered the paneled walls and heavy maroon drapes in the office, the portrait of George V amid the shadows, which somehow denied that this was B.G. and that there was a torpid sun outside.

Orly had given him a week in which to decide and it was then that he had taken the trip into the bush. It was to have been an overland trek to Kaieteur Falls deep in the interior and he had taken two friends, a guide and Sybil—since his

wife had already left for America. Early in the
trip, when they had stopped because of the heat,
he had wandered alone into the bush surrounding
their camp, curious to know what it would be like
away from the marked trail they were following.
Slowly, as he had moved over the thick under-
brush, parting the tangled branches and looped
vines which hung like a portiere before him, he
had sensed it. The bush had reared around him
like the landscape of a dream, grand and gloomy,
profuse and impenetrable, hoarding, he knew,
gold and fecund soils and yet, somehow, still rav-
enous. So that the branches clawed at him, the
vines wound his arms, roots sprang like traps
around his feet and the silence—dark from the
vast shadows, brooding upon the centuries lost
—wolfed down the sound of his breathing. He
had felt a terror that had been the most exquisite
of pleasures and at his awed cry the bush had
closed around him, becoming another dimension of
himself, the self he had long sought. For the first
time this self was within his grasp. If he pursued
this dark way long enough he would find it hanging like a jeweled pendant on the trees—and it
would either shape his life by giving him the
right answer to Orly's offer or destroy him.

But then he had heard Sybil—and she might
have been the sane and cautious part of himself
coming to save him; indeed, he had come to believe
this over the years—a twig snapping under her

step and her puzzled voice in the stillness. "Gerald . . . ?"

He had turned to drive her away, but her expression had stopped his angry gesture and her eyes, which she had inherited from her part-Chinese father—swift, prescient, set at a slant in her dark face—gazed past him to the bush ahead. She clearly saw what he had only glimpsed and understood better than he ever would its danger, and with a protective cry she had rushed forward and placed herself between him and what could have been a vision of himself.

"Come, man," she had said, her hand insistent on his sleeve. "Let's get out this damn jungle." And he had followed her back to the camp, hating her for the first time.

That night Sybil had complained of feeling ill and had asked to be taken home. The next morning they had started back to Georgetown. The following week Gerald Motley had accepted the job with B.G. Broadcasting, assuring his success. Shortly after he had begun stopping at the King George Bar across from his office for a drink each morning and spending his evenings at Ling's on Water Street.

He was in Kitty Village now, an old suburb that was really part of Georgetown. The houses huddled on their stilts above the eddying mud would be filled, he knew, with the smell of mold and mildew, damp bodies and water-soaked wood and

smoke from the kitchen fires. But this no longer
mattered, for the rain had given way to the ad-
vancing sun and a small girl, her skirt tucked
between her legs, was laughing as she fished a
drowned hen from the flood, and a black woman
sang as she washed clothes under a house. Everywhere the shutters were propped open to welcome
the first dry wind.

Gerald Motley stopped the car in front of a
house where a tall coconut palm still dripped in
the front yard, and straightening the trousers of
his expensive cream-colored linen suit, tightening
the belt over the thick flesh at his waist, he settled
down to wait. He watched the child pursuing the
drowned hen, sharing her tension and excitement.

He had finished two cigarettes, the child had
gone off triumphantly with her hen, when a young
man of about twenty-five appeared on the steep
flight of sagging steps which led from the house to
the yard. At first glance he looked no different
from a minor clerk in the government service. A
part cleaved his rough hair down the middle like a
narrow track through a jungle. He wore a white
shirt and a tie, but no jacket, and a watch, a
harsh, cheap gold against his black wrist. He was
ready, it seemed, for a day sifting papers in an
airless office.

But his manner denied this. He stood, a slender,
dark hand at his waist, scowling down at the
flooded yard and ignoring Gerald Motley, who

waited below. Frowning, he finally descended, tall
and slim-hipped, his shoulders drawn in slightly
as if he disliked being touched. There was a subtle
contempt in each small gesture and a disdain in
his lidded eyes which, since he was so young, only
betrayed his helplessness. He leaped across the
drainage trench to the car and, as he almost
slipped in the mud, his hand reached up in a gesture of anger and disgust which would have hauled
down the sky if possible.

Five years ago the young man, Sidney Parrish,
had won a scholarship to study in England; then
his father, a stevedore, had been killed in an accident on the docks and, as the oldest of many children, he had had to remain in B.G. and work. He
had come to B.G. Broadcasting for a job and, as
he got into the car now, Gerald Motley remembered him standing at his desk that first day, his
anxiety showing beneath a thin armor of arrogance. Gerald Motley had hired him because he
had glimpsed something about himself in the boy's
cold stare, and he had kept him on since, in a way
he could not know, the boy became the part of
him which refused to spare him the truth, which
remained always critical and unforgiving.

Gerald Motley had been grateful for this, and
to prove it he had promoted Sidney frequently.
With each promotion Sidney had become more
distant and contemptuous, and then openly in-
solent. And Gerald Motley encouraged this dis-

respect. Two years ago, he had started buying Sidney's drinks and lunch, and more recently he had started driving him to work and taking him along to Ling's in the evening and to the elite Georgetown parties. He had even taken him once to a reception at Government House. Sidney, for his part, repaid this generosity, fed it, with his scorn and abuse.

"Oh, Christ, man, see if you can't drive without trying to wreck the car for a change. My head feels like the drum that chap at Ling's was beating last night," Sidney said, and rested his head against the back of the seat.

"Be glad it's your head, boy, and not your gut. That's when you can start worrying." And then as Sidney closed his eyes, he added quickly, "How was the little craft you had in tow when you left Ling's last night?"

"Don't ask," Sidney said with weariness and disgust. "The craft drank more Russian Bear rum than you and me put together and stayed sober the whole bloody night. So that every time my hand would reach for the goods she was pushing it away. I finally had to get out the pacifier." With his eyes closed he reached in his pocket and held up a small white pill, which he dropped deftly into his other hand as if into a glass. "This in a Black Velvet finally did it."

Gerald Motley glanced at the pill and then at the slim, perfect line of Sidney's throat, his taut flesh, and thought of his own flesh, which was heavily creased and hanging in great folds over his frame. He sat up and held in his stomach. "How was she?" he asked.

"The bitch had skin like cold fat."

Their laughter floated across the traffic and was lost, and Gerald Motley had to press the brake as one of his long, curved fenders nudged a donkey cart loaded with sugar cane. The driver of the cart had been asleep at his whip, but he awoke now and turned angrily; then as he saw the Jaguar and glimpsed Gerald Motley's pale face through the windshield, he hastily lifted his cap, gave the pained smile of deference and turning back began flailing his donkey.

Gerald Motley swept by with an apologetic wave and, pressing a way through the slow-moving pack of lorries, cars and bicycles, reached downtown Georgetown, the part of the city which had been rebuilt after the great fire of 1945. The unsightly drainage trenches had been hidden under an island of grass and flamboyant trees in the middle of the wide main road, the government buildings, large shops and offices set well back from the sidewalks and painted a flat, unnatural white, so that at noon, when the sun was a single hot eye within the empty face of the sky, Georgetown became a city of chalk, without shadows.

Sidney was asleep by the time they reached the offices of B.G. Broadcasting, and after he parked

Gerald Motley also rested his head against the back of the seat. He thought he saw the dampness and heat rising in a thick steam from the concrete road. He felt the perspiration secreting itself in the cracks of his dried skin, under the sweatband of his Panama hat. His linen suit would be wilted within the hour.

He looked up at the air conditioner in his office window and muttered with an amused and despairing smile, "A blasted air conditioner which hasn't worked in over four months, because the only person in the whole of the colony who can fix it is sick in hospital. That's what we call progress in B.G." He turned to Sidney. "Up and out, boy, and, oh, Christ, don't forget the Tide commercial again today."

He left Sidney in the car and, pitching slightly as if he had already had the drink, crossed the road to the King George Hotel. The bar was to the back and it had been built of woven palm fronds lashed to a bamboo frame, so that it always held, as if it were a reservoir, the cool, dry solemnity of nights in the dry season. Gerald Motley stood in the middle of the room, breathing the coolness and smiling at the sunlight which had edged in through the palm leaves and lay in golden scales across the floor. Standing there, swaying slightly, he somehow resembled the houses he had passed on his morning drive into the country. Like them his legs seemed too weak to sustain his weight. At any moment they might buckle and he would come crashing down.

He clapped and the old Hindu waiter emerged from behind the bar, as swift and silent as the shadows there. "Is you, Mr. Motts," he said, and began pouring the drink.

He brought it to Gerald Motley between trembling hands and stood beside him while he drank, his white hair flaring around an ancient face that had been sucked in around the bones so that he resembled a fakir. His clotted eyes gazed up at Gerald Motley with a strange sorrow and reproof.

"It's true, sir, everything is changing up," he said, taking the empty glass, and he might have been resuming a conversation they had had yesterday or a year ago. "It's raining now when it ought be dry. And come time for the rain we'll have drought instead. People don't know when to plant little rice any more."

"Ah, Singh . . ." Gerald Motley said softly, remembering the Hindu family standing in their ruined rice field that morning.

"The paper says it's the bombs the Yankees are dropping in the sea for practice that's got things so turned around. Well, I guess we ought to be glad they ain't practicing on us yet. . . ." His laugh, a thin, toneless wheeze, blew the flecked sunlight across the floor.

"Ah, Singh." Gerald Motley touched his shoulder and was glad to find it so warm, so

charged with life under the fragile bone. Singh's
agelessness was the small part of Gerald Motley
which would remain ageless.

"Don't worry, old man," he said, and patted
the shoulder. "You don't know it, but you're living in the safest place on God's earth. The
Yankees won't be dropping any bombs here because they've never even heard of a place called
B.G. In fact, nobody is quite certain of our existence except a few chaps in the Colonial Office
and they don't count. . . ."

Gerald Motley remained a little longer, listening to Singh's fears and nodding while the rum
eased the gnawing in his stomach and seeped his
blood; then he left, taking the coolness of the bar
with him into the surging heat outside. He was
halfway across the road when he paused suddenly
under a flamboyant tree on the island of grass over
the trench and, staring across at his office window
and the useless air conditioner there, he was re-
luctant to begin the morning's work. He would
have liked to hold back the day, to gain time. He
wanted suddenly to return to the bar, which ex-
cluded time, and to Singh, who had escaped it. He
would be safe there, he sensed. From what? He
did not know. Whatever it was had been contained in the boys' shouted warning that morning.

He had turned back toward the bar when a
large white Opel Kapitan stopped him at the curb
and the driver, a dark, heavy woman with graying

hair and wearing a rumpled doctor's coat, called out to him, "Get out the road, Motts, and know you're obstructing traffic."

"Ah, Murie-mine," he said, laughing, and leaning down kissed the puffy arm propped on the window. "Let the patient die and come have a grog with me."

"I can't stop."

"Only one, Murie, it'll make your hand steadier on the knife."

"Yes, just as yours is steady," she said, and glanced piercingly at his hands as though she could see the twitching of each fine nerve within the thick flesh.

"One."

"You hear, I can't stop!" she cried, laughing. "I've got to pick up the children from school, get out to the airport and be back at the hospital all in an hour's time."

"Who're you meeting out at the airport?"

"Sybil," she said, and the pause was imperceptible before she added, "She's coming down on holiday."

Beneath the surprised laugh he quickly summoned, the uneasiness of a moment ago returned, stronger this time, and the wariness crouched behind his eyes.

"Sybil, eh?" he said. "So the old girl finally decided to give us a shout."

"Almost twenty years," Murie said.

It seemed longer, for he had forgotten that this stout, successful matron was Sybil's sister and that they had once even looked alike, with the same fine bones set at a slight tilt under the dark skin and eyes like two swiftly moving crescents of light. They had both been slender and quick, although Sybil had also been capable of a lovely stillness that had been like a dancer pausing after a leap. He had met them just after their return from the university in England (like most of the Chinese in B.G., their father had owned a large shop and had died indulging them). Gerald Motley had been almost forty then, Murie thirty and Sybil somewhat younger. As black women who had been to university they were rarities in B.G. and they had used this. Murie, shrewd and tireless, had built a successful practice and then married into a leading high-colored family which had lost its money and whom she now ruled, ruthlessly, with her money, while Sybil had been the first colored reporter for the *Georgetown Herald*, but unlike Murie she had never settled in, but had remained somehow remote, restless and lonely.

Thinking of her now as he chatted about her with Murie and tried to shape her face out of the shifting memories, Gerald Motley could only really remember the quality of her loneliness. It had been as much a part of her smell as the cologne she had used; it had often lent a fierce and excessive note to her laughter, and it had always brought on her rages during the long rain. It had been his loneliness, and the loneliness and despair of the land. Even now, on nights when he had not had enough to drink and Sidney had gone off early with a woman, he would feel it—like an alien wind hiding in the acacia trees around his house. . . .

"How do you think the old girl looks after all this time?" he asked, and smiled as Murie scrutinized him from behind her sunglasses.

"Old," she said flatly. "Just as you're old, and me, for that matter."

"I mean . . ."

"I know what you mean," she said with a sudden roughness and impatience. "She's probably the same damn Sybil. Look how I didn't get the cable that she was coming until last night. Well, thank God, the rain stopped. You know how she hated this place when it rained. Want to ride out to the airport with me?"

He felt a tremor jar his heart and hid his reluctance behind a laugh. "There's nothing I'd like more than to be part of the welcoming committee, dear Murie, but I haven't even been to the office yet."

"But I'm sure you've been over to your other office already." She waved toward the hotel bar. "All right," she said, and started the motor. "Just make sure you come over to the house tonight. I'm having in what's left of the old crowd to give her a real Guianese welcome. She'll probably curse me good and proper for doing it. As for you, I suppose you'll be bringing along your bodyguard."

"Ah, Murie, I'm a man beset by enemies and must be heavily guarded at all times. . . ."

"Beset by your own damn self, you mean. Well, just tell Sidney Parrish not to come in my house looking as if he smells something bad." The car lurched into motion and she was gone.

She would be exhausted by the time she reached the airport and irritable, he thought, and felt his own sudden exhaustion and irritability at the thought of Sybil's coming as he climbed the stairs to his office. The main office through which he had to pass held the dampness of every rainy season, the oppressive heat and dust of a drought and the mingled odors of the clerks who worked there. A toneless fugue of "Morning, Mr. Motley" trailed him to his private office and the guarded glances above the rattling typewriters told him that they knew he had stopped for the drink and that they both envied him and disapproved.

He opened his office door and his secretary looked up from her idle typewriter, her face ghostly with the whitish powder she used to make her dark skin lighter, her eyes moist with the thought of the flowered yard goods she had seen in Woolworth's window on her way to work.

"Morning, Mr. Motley. Mr. Orly called."

"What in the bloody hell did he want?" He carefully hung up his jacket and absently shuffled the papers on his desk, feeling the grit of weeks on his fingers.

"He wanted to know if you were making arrangements to tape the governor's speech on the Queen's birthday."

"And did you tell Frank Orly, O.B.E., S.O.B., that we don't need him to remind us of something we've been doing for the past twenty years?"

"No, I didn't tell him all that, sir, I just said we had arranged for it."

"Well, if he calls again, Miss Davis, you tell him what I just said."

"Yes, sir, Mr. Motley."

"Is there anything else of equal urgency?"

"No, sir, Mr. Motley."

"Then come, girl, let's hear who died last night."

"Oh, dear, I almost forgot the time," she cried, excitement edging her voice as she turned on the radio.

A hymn emerged from the static: "Abide with me/Fast falls the eventide . . ."

" 'The darkness deepens,' " Gerald Motley sang, and Miss Davis clasped her hands over her chest pressing back her shock and laughter. The music receded and Sidney's voice loomed—grave, sonorous, deeper than it was ordinarily, coming, it seemed, not from the speaker but through the slats of the closed shutters and creating shadows which stood like mourners around the room.

He would be slouched in front of the micro-

phone in the studio upstairs, refusing to touch the
sheet of paper which listed the names of the dead,
Gerald Motley knew. He listened to the subtle
anger beneath Sidney's soothing voice and
watched Miss Davis, who sat with her head bowed
as though she was at devotions. He heard her small
gasp each time Sidney paused dramatically before giving the next name and then her breath
rushing out as he spoke it—and Gerald Motley
knew that like himself Miss Davis was only certain of being alive in the midst of the dead.

". . . We regret to announce the demise of
Millicent Dembo of Salamander Road, Kitty Village, the beloved mother of fifteen and the revered
grandmother of sixty and great-grandmother of
well over a hundred, who passed peacefully in her
sleep last night at the age of ninety-five. . . ."

It was the last name. The music rose, then
faded, and Sidney began the commercial for Tide
in his normal voice. Miss Davis stirred; her shoulders flickered with annoyance. "Nobody interesting today, sir," she said, half turning to Gerald
Motley. "But at least Mr. Parrish didn't forget
Tide again."

Gerald Motley started to nod, but instead his
head gave a slight shudder and dropped, and the
cigarette he was smoking fell from his hand. It
was not Miss Davis or her remark which jarred
him. He always forgave her because he considered
her no more than the part of himself which had

remained callous and mean-spirited and filled with an abstract resentment. Rather, it was the thought of the old woman who had died last night. He might have passed her many times on the road through Kitty Village. Suddenly he was sure that he had. He remembered her—an old woman with shriveled flesh and eyes thick with cataracts leading a gaunt cow to pasture.

He rose, pushing aside the papers. "Telephone across to the hotel if anything comes up."

"Yes, sir, Mr. Motley."

This time he sat on the patio which opened off the King George bar, his sodden bulk in the wilted linen suit sprawled in a low chair. He listened to a shrike in the palm trees which walled the patio and waited for Singh to bring him the drink, but before Singh could come he had nodded off, a dream stumbling across the troubled surface of his mind. In the dream the shrike's piercing-sweet cry became a siren's call which urged him through the deserted streets of Georgetown at night, through a swirling yellow fog of heat to the empty house where his wife had once lived. He ran through rooms which no longer had walls between them, searching for her, until he came to the servants' quarters in the back yard. There he found, not his wife, but Sybil, her face covered with a whitish powder and a flamboyant blossom growing from her mouth. Beneath the shroud she wore, her body above the waist was that of an old woman with shriveled flesh and dry flapping dugs and, below, the lithe, pleasing form of a young boy.

"Did you hear your blasted Tide?"

He was instantly awake, the dream forgotten. "Yes, my boy, and you gave your usual moving performance. Have a grog." He clapped for Singh. "There was only one thing wrong with to-day's announcements according to my secretary. There wasn't anybody really interesting, she said."

"What about the old woman in Kitty Village ninety-five years old? Think of the funeral, man! The weeping and wailing of the fifteen head of children and the hundred-and-sixty-odd grands and great-grands. Think of the women at the funeral dressed up in white like the Foolish Virgins. And the cars lined up from here to Kitty Village. The rum flowing . . ." Sidney broke off.

"Yes, that one impressed me too, but I think Miss Davis wants big names."

"That ghoul. She sucks blood, you know. You can tell from her eyes."

Gerald Motley's laugh drowned out the shrike and as he fell back in the chair, his body rigid in the paroxysm of the laugh, Sidney hunched forward, unsmiling, and drank the rum which Singh had placed before him and then very carefully set the glass into the wet ring it had formed on the table.

"Blast her in hell," he said quietly and then, with his eyes closed, "and blast me for sitting there each and every day taking the name of the dead in vain to the tune of 'Tide's In.' You think they'd have this rotten business on a station in New York or London?"

"They've got worse there," Gerald Motley said, suddenly sobering. "But at least the chaps there are making big money and can afford a decent grog to wash the bad taste out their mouths and a time with a good-looking craft to help them forget. But what is our reward in this God-forsaken patch of Her Majesty's Empire—yours for singing the praises of the dear departed, mine for kissing Frank Orly's pink ass all these years and his father's before him? Nothing but Russian Bear rum giving us cirrhosis of the liver, a few syphilitic sailor hags down on Water Street giving us paresis to the brain and an equatorial heat." He downed the last of his drink. "But you know what the real trouble is with B.G.?"

"No, what is it today?"

"Ah, Sidney," Gerald Motley chuckled, pleased. "There's no pity in you, boy, and no respect, and that's a good thing. It makes me feel young, since only the old are to be pitied and respected."

"What is it?"

"The bush."

The word uttered with a lingering sibilance

seemed to bring that immense and brooding tract suddenly close, so that both Sidney and Gerald Motley glanced at the wall of palm trees, Sidney frowning and strangely irritated, Gerald Motley smiling ruefully and thinking that with Sybil's return that day in the bush had also returned. He sat back in his chair now and said quietly, "That's the real B.G. and until something is done with it nothing else about the colony will matter."

"Oh, Christ, what's this about the bush all of a sudden?" Sidney said, and snatched up Gerald Motley's cigarettes. "Last night at Ling's you were getting on about the same thing."

"Was I?" he said, and strained in his mind to separate last night from all the other nights. "I don't remember."

"You were too damn salt to remember."

Gerald Motley's laugh reached into the bar, to Singh, who peered at him through the dimness with the same sad reproof.

"The bush!" Sidney stabbed out with the cigarette. "What bush? Tell me, you ever went near the blasted place?"

"Yes."

"And?"

But Gerald Motley had answered too quickly and could find no way of telling him what had happened, too eagerly, for Sidney was suddenly suspicious. They waited in a silence loud with the battling of two flies around the mouth of Gerald

Motley's glass, until finally he said lightly, "It was years ago on a trip to Kaieteur. We didn't get very far though before we had to turn back because the rains started up. . . ."

He wished that the cigarette Sidney held was a whip Sidney would use to scourge him for the lie. He added casually, "Before I forget, we're going to a spree at Murie Collins' tonight. She's giving it for her sister, who's flying in from Jamaica today. The sister, by the way, was one of the people on this trip to Kaieteur years ago. You might have heard her name. Sybil Jeffries. She used to be with me at the station when I first started. She's assistant to the program director for Radio Jamaica now and doing damn well, I hear."

"I know all about her," Sidney said. "I also know that you went around with her for years but you wouldn't marry her, even when you could, because she was black and her father was only a shopkeeper—and that's why she finally left B.G."

The thrust was well aimed and deep and the pain perfect. Gerald Motley smiled gratefully and said, "I see you've been talking to my enemies. Yes, that was partly it. You can put up your knife. Regrettably, Sidney, I come from a bastard breed that once considered itself highborn. But there were other, more important reasons . . ." and could not confess that whenever he had slept with Sybil she had not only brought her body and laid that beside him, but her loneliness also, stretching it out like a pale ghost between them, and her intense, almost mystical suffering, asking him silently to assuage it. But she had asked too much. He would have had to offer up himself to do so, and he refused. Nor could he admit to Sidney the most important reason: that he had never forgiven her for having denied him that vision of himself that day in the bush.

"Come, let's have some lunch." He rose heavily.

Upstairs in the hotel dining room the closed shutters did not succeed in barring the noon heat, and the fans droning louder than the flies, the potted ferns and white walls and tablecloths failed in the illusion of coolness. As soon as the waiter finished serving them, Sidney said, "Was I invited tonight or am I just being taken along for effect?"

Gerald Motley put down his fork and waited, a smile forming.

"I just want to know whether I should thank you or Murie Collins," Sidney said, and pushed aside his untouched plate.

Gerald Motley glanced at the food he would pay for, at the dark hand poised on the white tablecloth as if to strike him and his smile broadened. He drank half of his gin and tonic before he said, "Don't thank anybody. Just come. The grogs'll be flowing and that's all that matters. There might even be one or two crafts your age about the place . . ."

Sidney nodded. "You've told me. Thanks. I

didn't think it was Murie Collins, who doesn't speak to me unless I'm with you. And why should she speak; after all, I'm not in the league of the great." His sarcastic gesture took in Gerald Motley and the others in the dining room. Aside from a few English planters and businessmen and Portuguese merchants perspiring over the heaped rice and overfried steak on their plates, and an occasional wealthy East Indian and Chinese, the majority were the colored and black professionals, politicians and highly placed civil servants of Georgetown, most of them as dark as Sidney; there were now only a few left as fair as Gerald Motley.

"After all," Sidney was saying quietly, "I don't live in a big house on Dodds Road, nor do I drive a long expensive car, nor do I wear white linen suits. And I don't look white. My father and his father were like so." He raised a dark, angry hand. "And he worked on the docks, man, and died there in some bloody, senseless accident. And my house?" He gave a sudden wild laugh which was like a lament. "But then you've seen my house. As for me, I'm just a two-shilling-a-week announcer and that only by the grace of my benefactor and for his amusement."

He sat back, distraught beneath his calm, cruel and somehow old, staring coldly at Gerald Motley and through him at the others in the room. Then, although his eyes didn't change, he laughed again, a loud, boyish burst this time, which flung back his head to reveal the perfect line of his throat.

"Oh, Motts, I'm going to the damn spree," he said. "I just wanted to make my position clear."

Gerald Motley closed his eyes for a moment to shut out Sidney's pain. The perspiration was like guilty tears on his face and he bowed his head. Finally, when he was certain that his hand was steady again, he picked up his fork and when he was sure of his voice, he gave the old laugh and said, "Well, then, let's eat, boy. I'm hungry from your talking."

After lunch Sidney returned to the station and Gerald Motley remained at the hotel, in hiding from the sun which had usurped the sky by now. Each noon it was as if Singh's fear was made flesh: the Yankees had dropped the bomb. For the heat then, searing white on the chalk-white buildings, must have been similar to that which comes at the moment of a massive explosion. The glare offered even the blind of Georgetown a vision of the apocalypse and the weighted stillness mushrooming over the city was the same which must follow a bombing, final and filled with the broken voices of the dying. Georgetown at noon was another Hiroshima at the moment of the bombing, and the minor clerks in the government offices on Main Street wound their cheap watches to spur the afternoon; over at B.G. Local Broadcasting, Miss Davis rested her powdered forehead on the cool hump of her typewriter; upstairs in the studio Sidney read the praises of hot Ovaltine into the microphone and across the street Gerald Motley accompanied a few of the older colored professional men like himself down to the bar.

As always, their eyes offered him the image of his public self. For them, and for most of B.G., he was as Sidney had described him at lunch, a Motley—with his Panama hat and linen suits, his car—one of the few elite left. It did not matter that he had contradicted this image over the years by his long affair with Sybil Jeffries and the others after her, by his nightly visits to Ling's on Water Street and now, in his old age, by his attachment to Sidney. They forgave him all this and jokingly called Sidney his Aide-de-Camp. They insisted that he, Gerald Motley, was still one of them, indeed, better than them, and confirmed this whenever he joined them for an afternoon drink by a subtle show of deference. (Now one of them hurried over to Singh for a drink for him.) To them he was a success. It did not matter that he had done nothing outstanding at B.G. Broadcasting. What was important was that he had been the first colored man in the West Indies to hold such a position.

Seeing that image in their eyes, Gerald Motley closed his own eyes for a moment and wished that Sidney was hovering somewhere on the edge of the group so that he might look up and see the truth in

his cold stare. Then, with an ironic laugh, Gerald
Motley ordered drinks for them all, and to amuse
them he talked—his voice drowning out the
thought of the fleeting day and of Sybil, who
awaited him at its end.

". . . an army, gentlemen," he shouted at one
point. "That's another thing this colony needs.
And some guns. And once we get the army and
the guns, we must do one of three things. Either
invade Surinam to the east, declare war on Vene-
zuela to the west or provoke Brazil to the south.
That's the only way the world will ever know
there's a place called B.G. Or better yet, call on
the Russians. And then watch, gentlemen. Overnight we will have arrived! Uncle Sam will toss a
few million our way and the Queen herself will be
hotfooting it down here with some pounds. . . ."

Later, when the sunlight scattered along the
floor had softened, he was still talking, but now
the linen suit sagging from his shoulders defined
his sadness and his laugh was a ragged snatch between the words. "There's no hope, gentlemen,"
he was saying, but he was aware only of the cool,
moist surface of the glass Singh slipped into his
hand and the rum stinging his throat as he swal-
lowed. "The only solution to what ails B.G. is a
bomb at the heart of Georgetown. And *mirabile
visu*, our problems solved! An end to the P.P.P.,
the unholy triumvirate of poverty, politics (he
bowed to a member of the House of Assembly)

and prejudice which rules B.G. still. An end to a sun which burns our brains to an ash and a rain that drives us all to drink and delirium tremens. One bomb, gentlemen, and oblivion!" He finished his drink and clapped for Singh.

"And guess who'll come crawling out of the ashes," someone called.

"Motts, holding tight to a bottle of Russian Bear."

"You're damn right," Gerald Motley cried, and his laugh joined theirs. "And do you know why I'll survive, gentlemen? Because I'm the only one out of the lot of you who really loves the old place. I am B.G." And his extravagant gesture did seem to embrace the vast sweep of the land. "We're one and the same." He paused, thinking of his morning drives into the country and knowing suddenly that what he had sought all along had been the reflection of himself in each feature of the land. And he had been there, although he had not been able to see himself. The listing Hindu houses this morning had in some way reflected him, as had the family standing in their ruined field and the black men wielding their machetes among the gliding canes, the boys at their cricket.

"We're the same," he said, with an awed laugh.

A silence touched the room and he laughed again, a loud, echoing sound that scarcely resembled laughter and, bending over the bar, he stretched out his arms in the prostrate pose of a penitent before Singh, who waited on the other side with a drink for him. While he rested there and Singh held the rum over his head as if it were a holy oil he would use to anoint him in some final rite, the first breeze of the approaching evening came off the patio and sifted through the plaited walls. Gerald Motley felt its beneficence on his moist flesh and knew that there would be thin shadows slanting along the streets of Georgetown now and that the sun was groping, blinded by its own brilliance, down the western passage of the sky.

"Lemme leave you rum-heads," he said, straightening up. "Singh," he tossed some bills on the bar, "for the gentlemen's drinks."

"Old Motts," one of the men said affectionately. "We'll see you over to Murie's tonight."

"Hey, that's right," someone else said. "Motts's old craft is back. No wonder he's getting a little excited."

"Man, you best get in shape."

"Prime the instrument, Motts."

"All you do, go easy, because many an old man has breathed his last trying to run that race."

"Remember our reputation, Motts: studs second to none, and don't disgrace us."

He was borne across the room on their banter. He turned at the doorway and gazed at them with an affection ringed about with contempt. All of them except Singh were caught within this ring, including himself, for he was no different from them after all. He raised his hand, halting their amiable laughter, and said almost solemnly, "Hail, gentlemen, and farewell."

The thought of Sybil which had been muted inside the bar awaited him outside and followed him across the road and up the stairs to his office. She had been in the colony some hours now and he felt the pull of her presence as if he were joined to her by an invisible rope which she controlled. Each time she breathed or moved, he felt the slight pressure on the rope. Some fragment of the dream he had had on the patio nudged his mind— Sybil with withered breasts—and as he hurried through the empty main office (it was past four o'clock and the clerks and his secretary were gone, leaving only the studio upstairs open), he tried to drive out that image with the memory of her as a young woman. But even this was distasteful and he had to admit what he had long denied: that he had always been secretly offended by the lack of purity in her woman's form, the slight fullness to her breasts and hips. How would it be now that she was middle-aged? He closed the door to his office and spat into his handkerchief.

Sidney opened the door an hour later and paused, startled, at the sight of Gerald Motley at work on the papers piled on his desk. "How is it you're not cat napping as usual?" he asked, and did not wait for an answer. "Ready for a grog?" He held up the bottle of rum.

"No. Telephone across to the hotel for some tea."

"Tea?"

"Tea," he said sharply, and continued working.

Sidney stared closely at him for a moment and then left. He returned after some time with a waiter from the hotel who brought in the tea on a tray. But the teapot remained under its cozy and the cup stayed empty as Gerald Motley worked on. Sidney sat on the window ledge, drinking from the bottle of rum, which was a blaze of amber in the abrupt tropic sunset, and staring gloomily down at the deserted streets.

As dusk invaded the room, he turned toward Gerald Motley with an inexplicably sad and angry motion. It was as if the silence between them and Gerald Motley's absorption in the work on his desk, as well as the night burgeoning above the distant bush, had brought on his despair. He stared at Gerald Motley with a profound and abstract bitterness. His eyes became mere slivers in his dark face, his look that of a man watching another die with utter dispassion.

"Well, let's hear it," Gerald Motley said, and put aside the last of the finished papers before he looked up.

"Hear what?"

"The announcement you're busy composing. Mine, isn't it?"

"You and your damn secretary have the same ghoulish turn of mind." Sidney turned back to the window.

"Let's hear it. 'We regret . . .' "

"I'm through work for the day." Sidney rose quickly. "You'll have to wait until tomorrow."

Chuckling, Gerald Motley followed him from the office down into the street, past the shuttered buildings and shops into the wind which bore the night through the city. They were headed, as on every evening at this time, to Water Street and Ling's.

Ling's was one of the sailor clubs which cluttered Water Street. Like all the others it was always filled with the idle of Georgetown, the cheap thieves and cozeners, the petty gamblers and touts of the race track, the panderers for the sailors who might wander in, the brawlers and sots— the veins of their eyes gorged with blood and radiating in amber spokes from the dark centers. Curses flouted the hushed and sacred night outside, and the laughter, thick as the heat, was a hosanna to the pin-up goddesses from America hanging on the walls.

Ling herself presided from a high stool near the cashbox behind the bar, her one good eye resting maternally on her customers, her head cocked

toward the breeze of a sluggish fan and nodding to
the noise—an old bawd she was, with a gelid glass
eye and a stomach swollen with tumors, whom
Gerald Motley loved, for in a way which he
could never know, she had become the part of him
which had gazed upon the darkness within and
found it pleasing. . . .

"But, Ling, my love, when are you going to
drop that child, eh?" he leaned across the bar and
tapped the huge belly.

"Soon, God willing, Mr. Motts. It's an immacu-
late conception, you know. A damn Chinee Jesus."
The stomach shuddered with her laugh and pouring them a drink she began the familiar recital of
her ailments: "But it's not the stomach so much
any more; the blasted arthritis is the thing that's
got me going nowadays. . . ."

Usually they would stay only long enough for
this single drink with Ling and then leave, returning later on in the night for the last rum with her
before going home. But tonight Gerald Motley
left Sidney behind at the bar with Ling and wandered around the crowded room, greeting the
familiar faces there and pouring drinks from a
bottle of expensive whisky he had bought from
Ling.

As he penetrated into the violent center of the
crowd and felt the intimate press of their bodies
against his and the hands clawing at his arm for
the bottle, as the warm yeast smell of their

sweated, unwashed bodies overwhelmed him and the noise roared like a rough sea in his ears, he felt rid of himself: of his old man's body, that sodden, slow-moving hulk he hid in expensive linen suits, of his face which had come to remind him of a reflection seen in a trick mirror where all the features appear to thicken and dissolve, of his mind which had grown barren waiting for the seed.

Freed of this single self, he became those around him. He was the thief whose hand glanced his pocket as he passed, the panderer whispering as he did every night, "A nice coolie girl just up from the country, Mr. Motts, a guaranteed virgin," the tout muttering a hunch on the next day's race as Gerald Motley poured him the drink, the beggar counting the day's spoils in a corner. . . .

"Are you still going to the spree or what?" Sidney's voice was a cold prod which roused him from where he sat, half-asleep, among a group of gamblers.

"And have you ever known me to miss a spree?" he said, groping up, his hand reaching for Sidney, who quickly moved away. A laugh rattled like phlegm in Gerald Motley's throat. "What did I say about pity," he said, wagging a finger. "Come, let's be off and change. After all, we can't go to Murie Collins' smelling under the arms. I'll drive to my place; then you take the car and go home and dress, and come back for me."

On the way out he leaned over to kiss Ling and as he did, her glass eye seemed curiously alive and filled with a yellow light which probed him deep; slowly the light changed, becoming somber and gray with concern. In that fragile moment, while the light altered, a chill struck Gerald Motley's muscles so that he could not move; then, as quickly, he laughed and kissed her again.

"Ling, my love, we'll be back for our nightcap."

"God willing, Mr. Motts," she said, and the glass eye went blank.

With Sidney strangely tense and silent beside him, Gerald Motley walked back to B.G. Broadcasting for the car and, once settled behind the steering wheel, he sped through Georgetown, chasing the night, which seemed to be racing now toward midnight, eluding him, just as the day which he had hoped to hold back had eluded him.

When they reached his house on Dodds Road, Sidney took over the wheel as Gerald Motley got out of the car and drove off without breaking his silence.

The Motley house reared like a high, white, stilted monument in the darkness, its closed shutters hiding rooms where the last echoes had long been stilled. As usual, the servant had left a light within and Gerald Motley followed its faint glow down the long stale passages, through the close cavernous rooms of silent clocks and faded antimacassars, calling her.

"Medford!" He pulled off his limp jacket for her to take. "Medford."

She usually appeared almost immediately, a thin, black, severe form, as ageless as Singh was ageless, her head wound in a silk kerchief printed with the Statue of Liberty which her daughter had sent her from America. But tonight he had to call several times before he heard her slurred tread and, when she emerged around the corner of a dim passage, he saw that she was dressed in white with a white straw hat instead of the kerchief. As she hobbled toward him—her face, arms and ancient legs lost in the shadows—she might have been an apparition.

"Where're you going this time of night?" He impatiently flung her the jacket and his hat.

"I'm not going, I'm just now coming, but I was gone for the whole day," she said with measured defiance. "My friend from years back died and I was to the funeral . . ." He abruptly walked away and she followed him, still talking. "Did you hear Mr. Parrish give the announcement this morning about a Millicent Dembo in Kitty Village? That was my friend. She had a hard life but a sweet funeral. You never saw so many cars, Mr. Motts. And Millie made such a pretty dead. I helped dress her the morning. But you know something, Mr. Motts"—she was standing in the doorway of his bedroom now, the linen jacket trailing down from her lax hand—"her limbs was still loose when I was washing her and she was still warm, even though she had passed early the night before. And they say when you see a dead come like that, the limbs soft and limber so and warm, you can always look for somebody else to dead soon."

"Oh, Christ, woman!" He turned irritably and then paused. Behind her innocent and murky gaze he thought he suddenly glimpsed himself as a boy. It was as if Medford had kept, and would always keep, the memory of his boyhood safe— and, thus, somehow alive. Humble suddenly, again the boy begging her forgiveness for some misdeed, he said gently, "Ah, Medford, mark my words, you're going to turn into a *bacoo* yet. Come, get out some clean clothes for me and stop with your foolishness. Come!" He clapped, startling her. "I was due at a spree hours ago. I'm keeping a lady waiting."

By the time he had bathed and dressed and drunk the small glass of rum which Medford brought him, Sidney returned. He had not changed his clothes and, as Gerald Motley walked toward the car, Sidney got out and handed him the keys.

"I'm not going to the spree," he said. "I've called up a craft and arranged to meet her in town instead."

"Oh," Gerald Motley said, and waited.

"To hell with Murie Collins' spree! And to hell with your damn Lady Sybil from Jamaica. It's your bloody funeral, not mine."

There was a moment's disbelief and then Gerald Motley laughed, "Ah, Sidney, did I ever accuse you of having no pity? I was wrong, boy. You are the soul of pity. And that almost disappoints me. Not only that, you're wise, boy. Come, I'll drive you to meet the craft. Which is it? Not the one from last night with skin like cold fat."

They remained silent on the way to town, Sidney staring out the window and Gerald Motley watching the black road streak past the car as if it were a reel of film depicting his life—the events, the scenes, so blurred that nothing emerged and, thus, nothing mattered.

He opened the glove compartment and handed Sidney a flask of rum. "One for the road, boy."

Sidney took the flask and held it for some time before taking a drink. When he finally drank and passed it over, Gerald Motley felt the warm place where Sidney's hand had rested; as he fitted the mouth of the bottle to his he tasted Sidney there —and that taste and touch, so intimate somehow in the darkness, along with the rum searing his throat, restored him. The limp muscles across his back stiffened, the faint gnawing within his stomach ceased and he was ready suddenly for Murie's party and for Sybil.

By the time they reached the place where Sid-

ney was to meet the girl Gerald Motley was almost gay. He brought the car to a jolting stop and
as Sidney got out with a mumbled parting word,
he called after him, "I'll make quick work of this
spree and meet you at Ling's, so don't waste too
much time with the craft."

Sidney turned, his movement full of a surprise
he could not contain. Bending down he peered
across the short distance into the car, his hand
lifting in a tenuous gesture and his eyes, caught
by the light of a street lamp, revealing a sudden
solicitude and devotion beneath their cruelty. He
started toward the car as though he had changed
his mind and would accompany Gerald Motley
but he paused before completing the first step—an
invisible hand might have jerked him back—and
his own hand slowly dropped.

"At Ling's then," he said, and turned away.

Gerald Motley drove back the way he had come,
thinking of Sidney. He had felt just then the terrible weight of his youth, and the bitterness which
would waste him. He thought of him scowling
down at the flooded yard that morning, and of his
outburst at lunch, of the cheap watch he wore and
the girl he would not enjoy tonight, and was suddenly glad that he was old and almost finished
and would never know pain again.

Murie's house was on Dodds Road, near his, and
like his it was a white, towering relic raised on
stilts and secured behind a high stone wall with

bits of broken glass cemented into the top. Ferns
grew in baskets hung from the veranda roof, and
the hibiscus and bougainvillaea clustered round
the house mulled the air until it was like wine. Tonight the lighted windows were brilliants richly
displayed against the black sky, and the gay
voices and laughter rushing from the open windows seemed to ward off the night, keeping the
world safe till the morning.

Gerald Motley swung the car into the driveway,
its tires skidding as he made the turn without
slowing down, and sent it hurtling down the narrow aisle between the row of parked cars, past the
veranda where the overflow crowd from inside was
gathered under loops of yellow lights.

"There's Motts," someone called above the loud
pelleting of the loose gravel under the car and
Gerald Motley gunned the motor in a salute.

The only parking space was some distance from
the house, at the end of the driveway beyond the
reach of the veranda lights, under a saman tree
which was thick with the night as if with leaves.
The loose gravel settled under the car as he parked
it. The motor died. With his hand on the door,
Gerald Motley paused. The lights beyond and
the laughter suddenly wearied him. The thought
of the people there—Murie, who would chide him
for being late, Sybil, who would forgive him
again and again with her smile, all the others
whose eyes would offer him the false image of him-

self—oppressed him suddenly. He would have preferred Ling's. His hand started toward the steering wheel.

But it was too late for him to leave. He saw Sybil—a dark figure in a pale diaphanous dress who moved away from the crowd on the veranda to stand at the railing with her arms folded quietly and her face turned toward the darkness which hid him. He saw her turn once to call something to the others, saw her laugh with an easy lifting of her head. Then she slowly came down the veranda steps, across the yard and down the driveway between the parked cars. The hem of her dress flickered in the rush of light from a window and her heels raised little flurries of dust as they struck the ground.

It was the same step, but firmer and more resolute now—as if she came with a plan and would not be dissuaded—the same graceful form, but a little heavier and less fluid than he remembered it, and her shoulders, which had always been somewhat loose and sad, were set now, assured. Gerald Motley was certain, although he could not see her face, that this was not the Sybil of his dream on the patio, no old woman with dried breasts and blurred eyes. (He was relieved. This would make it less painful to look at her once they went into the light; his smile would be less false.) Rather, she seemed more the Sybil of his remembrance. Time was reversed suddenly. The years telescoped. The past, which had trailed and nettled him like a dog's tail, had been caught finally in the teeth of the present.

"But, Gerald, man, you drove in here as if you had a woman about to deliver on the seat next to you." She called while still a little distance away, her voice light and amiable, signaling him, it seemed, that she would be discreet and not restore the past or accuse him of old sins.

And grateful, he called back, "Is that Sybil loose in the land again?"

"Yes, man," she said, leaning down at the open window and pressing her face briefly against his. "Like the elephant I've come home to die."

Her skin was like stone that had been cooled and worn smooth by water passing over it, her fragrance the familiar one he had once carried home on his clothes and body every night. Her voice was the same. She had always unconsciously pitched it to the time of day. At night it would be hushed and driven deep in her throat as it was now, tense in the noon heat and listless during the rainy season. It was still young.

"You know that Murie is a lying brute. She told me Sybil was old," he said, slipping into the old bantering, indirect form of addressing her.

"She is," she said blithely, and stood up. "And tired. So open the car door and let her sit quietly for a minute before we go inside. Dear God!" she said, when she was settled on the seat beside him, her head resting on the back and a wide space between them. "This is the first rest I've known for the day. This morning it was the damn noisy plane, then Murie's rude children all afternoon and now this spree. . . ."

"It looks like we both need a grog then," he said and, finding a paper cup in the glove compartment, poured her a drink from the flask he and Sidney had used. As he sought her hand stretched toward him for the cup, he avoided looking at it or her face—even though they were both obscured by the darkness. He was afraid, absurdly so, that by some alchemy she had assumed her former self and was young again.

"You know," she said, taking the rum, "there's nothing worse than a welcome-home spree when you've been away as long as I have. It's like a bloody wake. You see all the old pack—or what's left of them—and you realize how old you are. Take Sylvan Hanes, for instance. Gerald, I scarcely knew Sylvan when he came up and spoke to me just now. And he's younger than I am, I know. And Dora. Look at Dora!"

"Didn't Murie write and tell you what happened to Dora?"

"No, man."

He told her and for a long time they spoke of Dora and the others they had known together, and of the dead, their voices easy and intimate in the night, their faces veiled. Both of them, as if by a silent pact, carefully avoided the question of themselves.

Finally, when there were no more names but theirs, she said, filling the silence, "Well, at least the old place hasn't changed. Orly and Company still own everything, I hear. The heat's the same. And the roads, especially that one from the airport, are still an abomination of mud. And the bush is still out there. We flew over it for miles and miles this morning. I never knew there was so much of it." Then, with a light, guilty laugh—as if she knew she was breaking their pact not to talk of each other—she said, "Tell me, did you ever try reaching Kaieteur Falls again?"

He felt a tightening across his chest and the need for a drink, for her question suddenly swept aside the intervening years and brought them both back to that time. He suspected, with a wariness which made his hand grope for the steering wheel, that she had never really moved beyond that time. Her years in Jamaica and her success there might have been nothing more than an attempt to forget those moments with him in the bush. And he had to admit, as he sat there trying to dismiss her question with a laugh as light as hers and a casual "No," that those moments were still vivid and urgent to him also. Perhaps neither of them had moved beyond that time and place. They might have left their selves behind among the trees and wandered in ghost forms down the

years. He felt like cursing her, like shouting as
he pushed her from the car and drove off that it
was unjust for her to return bringing the old
pain. He wished that he was at Ling's having a
rum and waiting for Sidney to come from the
woman.

"B.G. is the only place on God's earth you could
leave for a century and come back to find nothing's changed," she was saying, trying to restore
the pleasant tone, but as she continued talking her
voice slowly failed—and finally she broke off and
said, asking his forgiveness for the question with
a gesture hidden by the dark, "And what of you,
Gerald, man?"

He would have liked to have been able to recount
a long list of successes, thus proving to her that
despite her leaving he had been able to take hold.
And yet, on the other hand, he knew that he owed
her his failure. It would give her perhaps the comforting illusion that she had been crucial to any
success he might have had and that by refusing
to marry her he had brought on his ruin. His failure was the only way to make amends for having
refused her, the only way, perhaps, for him to
make amends for all his life: his privileged place,
his name, the wife and child he had driven
away. . . .

"Yes, what of me?" he said, with the laugh he
used to deny himself. "Well, you could say that
my life since Sybil left has been one slow decline

into rum and inertia. In the mornings and for most of the day there's Singh over at the King George Bar who ministers to my needs (he still asks for Sybil when he can remember that far back, by the way) and a lady named Ling at night who runs a bar on Water Street. It's not of a very high order, but then it's the only place in Georgetown that stays open all night.

"But don't mistake me, I work when I can spare the time. I'm still the puppet director at B.G. Broadcasting. But then, thank God, there's not much to direct since the program hasn't really changed since Sybil worked there and she and I had such grand schemes of making B.G. Broadcasting the voice of the West Indies. It's still cricket, news from the B.B.C. three times a day, the governor's speeches on the Queen's birthday and funeral announcements. That's the way Frank Orly and Company want it. But I can't say anything against Frank, you know. After all, he saves me the trouble of exerting myself in all this heat. The old boy has even installed an air conditioner in my office. It's yet to work properly, but it's there at least. No, Frank has been good."

He drank from the flask and remained silent for some time before he said, "Yes, and I still have the old place on Dodds Road and Medford still airs out the rooms once a week as though expecting company. What else, now? Oh, yes, about ten years ago I went up to England on my long leave, but I couldn't take the cold and fog. I still go over to Barbados once a year though and stretch out like a dead fish on the beach for a week or so. . . ." He turned to her, giving the little laugh, knowing its cruelty. "You mean to say Murie hasn't told Sybil all this in her letters? That doesn't sound like your sister."

The darkness had cleared a little so that he could make out her arm as it raised the cup to her lips.

She said quietly, "Yes, she's told me."

"Ah, I didn't think a Murie would miss the opportunity. Well, she's been busy because she's also kept me up to date on Sybil. I get full reports. I was informed of every step of Sybil's ascendency to power at Radio Jamaica, every detail of the big house with glass walls she built on a hill—what was it, five years ago?"

"Seven."

"And of course Murie told me about Sybil's getting married, but that was years ago now, and about the divorce. She said Sybil never told her what had happened though."

"Nothing happened. I got married too soon after I left here, that's all. After that I decided not to inflict myself on anyone again. No more marriage. I would just ask them to return my keys when I had had enough or tell the servant that I wouldn't be home to Mr. So-and-So any more and that was the end of it. But I've gotten too old for that." She gave a taut laugh. "You might say I don't go out in society any more."

Her voice had wandered listlessly over the words, refusing them all feeling and color, and now her sudden silence was so final she might have fallen asleep. As the moments passed and her breathing became inaudible, Gerald Motley had the curious feeling that she had vanished and it was Sidney asleep beside him as he had been that morning on the way to the office. She and Sidney seemed one and the same suddenly. And in an odd way they were. For although Sidney watched and waited for Gerald Motley's destruction to be complete and Sybil in her limitless compassion would have saved him if he had permitted her, the two things, his salvation and his end, were the same to him.

He glanced across at the still profile etched against the lesser blackness of the night, almost expecting to see Sidney there. But instead of that flawless line which Sidney's chin formed with his throat, he saw, dimly, the small sac of flesh, like a tremulous globule of water, beneath Sybil's chin.

He felt kindly toward her suddenly and sad about the husband she had lost and the score of lovers she had abandoned, for her body which had once pleased and impassioned him and now only filled him with distaste, for her memories which seemed drained of feeling (how well he knew about that!), above all, for whatever it was that had brought her back to B.G. Curious to know what this was, he said, "And so Sybil finally deigned to look up the old pack again."

"No, not the old pack, not even Murie so much. I came to see you," she said quietly, and he stiffened, offended, afraid that she would reach out and touch him, wanting to move further away from her. But, surprisingly, she was the one who moved deeper into her corner of the seat and folded her arms protectively over her breasts as if she was afraid he would touch her.

"It's about Radio Jamaica," she said, her voice stirring into life now. "Our program director is leaving. In fact, he's left by now. He was the usual white incompetent England dumps on her colonies and he couldn't half do the job. So I'm to be the new program director—Sybil's ascendency to power as you put it—but there's also been a new position created for someone above me who will coordinate the entire project. Of course, there was the usual talk about getting down someone from England, but I prevailed on them to look around the West Indies first. I suggested you and since they respect my judgment and knew your name, they asked me to come down and talk to you personally. . . ."

She was still talking when he started to laugh, and the sound, building into a small whirlwind, sucked up her words into its eye and spun with them from the car, through the trees and across

the yard to the veranda. A few people on the edge
of the crowd turned and peered toward the sound;
someone called inquiringly. But even when a
stout figure—Murie probably—came halfway
down the veranda steps and stared toward them,
Gerald Motley did not stop laughing. He could
not. The absurdity of her offer, its irony, convulsed him: life offering itself when there was
hardly any life left. It was a rare, grotesque
touch which appealed to his taste, the fitting coda
to his long day, and he wished that Sidney was
present to enjoy the moment with him.

"This calls for a drink," he said, reaching for
her cup and, as she waved aside the flask, he
added, "Oh, come, Sybil mustn't mind my laughing."

"It's all right," she said stiffly. "You always
laughed and said, 'This calls for a drink,' when
anything came up."

"Only when it wasn't anything serious, if you
remember."

"This is quite serious."

"Of course it is. It only becomes ridiculous, indeed ludicrous, when Sybil brings me into it. Perhaps she's forgotten the matter of my age."

"I know how old you are," she said quietly.

"And knowing that she would send me to do a
young man's job, have me leave a nice little air-
conditioned sinecure here to work like a coolie for
Radio Jamaica? She would have me spend what

little time is left to me in a heathen place where they don't even sell Russian Bear rum? Sybil isn't kind. Why how in the hell would I hold together without Russian Bear and the King George every morning and Ling's each night, without the old place, as hopeless as it is with the heat and the blasted rain, without the old pack inside." He motioned toward the house.

"Another thing"—and his voice had reached a savage pitch now—"who told Sybil I could co-ordinate anything? Not Murie certainly. She knows better. In all the years Sybil worked for me, did she ever see me do any co-ordinating or any directing for that matter—any work? So where then do I get all this experience she's claiming for me . . . ?"

"Oh, Gerald, stop going on, you could do the job." And her impatience was suddenly familiar. She had, how often in the past, urged him to something in just this way, not knowing as he had secretly known that it was not hesitancy or a lack of confidence on his part, but, simply, the terrifying awareness of his deficiencies.

His laughter was like the final agony, and he held out his hands in the dimness. "Sybil must let Murie tell her sometime how my hands shake these days," he said. Then: "No, I could not do the job. And even if I could I wouldn't. I'm afraid Sybil has put herself to all this trouble for nothing."

He was silent, his hands still raised between them. She was watching them, he knew, and then as if their tremor was contagious she began to tremble and her head slowly dropped in an eloquent gesture of defeat.

To seal that defeat, he said, "Sybil always had something of the missionary in her. She was always looking for souls to save."

"Oh, Christ, Gerald, but why have you always put me off so?" Her cry, full of rage and bewilderment, burdened the darkness and he knew suddenly—and his hands dropped—that she had waited all these years to ask the question.

He could have answered it but he didn't. He could have told her that he had never forgiven her for intruding between him and the discovery of himself that day in the bush. He could have said—if there had been words for it—that he had resented and feared the part of her love which had wanted to pool their suffering; above all, he could have confessed that although he had not known it then, he had found her woman's form distasteful.

But instead he said, "I'm sorry. I didn't mean to put Sybil off. In fact, I'm going to see to it that she doesn't go away altogether empty-handed. I can't find her a co-ordinator, but perhaps if Radio Jamaica needs an additional announcer I can be of some help. You see, I have a young chap by the name of Parrish on the staff who's really first-rate. There's no scope for him here though and no future. He does the funeral announcements and most of the commercials. We know where that will lead him in a few years. To the King George Bar and Ling's at night. I'd really like to see him get the chance to work for a big station like Radio Jamaica. Perhaps if Sybil is downtown tomorrow she will be kind enough to stop by the office and meet him. He was supposed to come tonight but was so overwhelmed, I think, by the prospect of meeting Lady Sybil—that's what he calls you— that he changed his mind at the last moment."

She turned slowly, her dress whispering at the movement, her voice as she spoke touched by an unnatural calm. "Wait, is this the boy Murie mentioned in her letter?"

His laugh exploded like a flare in the darkness. "Oh, God, that Murie! I should have known I could have depended on her. What did she write?"

"Something about a boy you're always walking about with as if he's a son or close friend or something so . . ."

"Or something so, eh? That sounds like Murie."

"She said that if people didn't know you they'd think something foolish was going on." She paused, waiting for his outrage and denial, for the laugh which would have cancelled all that Murie had implied.

When the laugh did not come, when he said nothing and his silence became an admission, she suddenly stiffened—and the air grew stiff—and, darting forward, she snatched up a book of matches which lay on top of the dashboard. She struck one, but it did not light—the sulfur was damp from the week's rain—and she flung it down. And another, her arm tracing a desperate arc in the dimness. Finally one caught and, cupping the small flame as though there was a wind, she leaned close and held it to his face.

He merely glanced at her through the flame and, finding what he had suspected—the worn flesh around the eyes, the subtle collapse of the tiny muscles beneath the skin which had drawn the skin down with them, the loneliness which had wasted her more than any disease and aged her faster than the years—he closed his eyes almost all the way and watched her from under his lowered eyelids.

Her mouth was tight with concentration, her eyes almost eclipsed by the heavy fold of flesh which gave them their Oriental cast; yet at the same time they seemed infinitely large, like huge elliptical mirrors which magnified his image so that he saw the old man who had once been her lover as clearly as she saw him, with his flesh arranged in slack folds which fluttered each time he breathed, his features so thickened they had lost their original forms, the skin discolored by his excesses. He could no longer be mistaken for white, or black for that matter, or East Indian. Over the years the various strains had cancelled out each other, it seemed, until he was a neuter.

She leaned closer, bringing the match so near he could hear the determined sputter of the flame as it edged down the damp stick and could feel its meager heat, and her eyes now probed within each crevice of his lined face and within the depth of his lidded eyes, finding there the confusion which had begun with his heritage, spread over the whole of his life and found its final expression in Sidney. The evidence was all there. And she saw something else which made her suddenly start and draw back and give a muted cry of fear and pity which made the small flame waver. It was, simply, the unmistakable form of his death lurking there—a death so imminent Gerald Motley would not be permitted to finish out the night, but would die in an accident on the road through Kitty Village into town.

All this was no more than the fraction of a moment, for the match quickly died, and in the silence a woman on the veranda laughed, a long, hysterical burst, the fitting response, it seemed, to some monstrous and eternal jest.

"Remember what the old people used to say?" Gerald Motley said, and his voice was light, gay. "That if you grant a man his last wish he dies easy and has a chance at heaven."

When she finally answered, her whisper was a thin quaver which betrayed her age. "All right,

Gerald, I'll come down to the office tomorrow and meet the boy. If he's really good I'll see what I can do. . . ."

"That does it then. Let's have one for the road."

"You're not stopping?"

"No, man, we've had our little chat. I'm sure Sybil can find some excuse to give Murie."

She allowed him to pour her a drink and then, with it poised near her lips, she said, her voice suddenly strong again, "This damn place. This damn, bloody place."

She got out of the car, leaving the door open behind her, and walked toward the veranda, where they were dancing now under the strung lights. She was still holding the paper cup of rum, bearing it gently between her hands as if the ash of his life was dissolved there.

"Remember me to Murie," he shouted after her, and gave the old irreverent laugh.

BRAZIL

Three trumpets, two

saxophones, a single trombone; a piano, drums
and a bass fiddle. Together in the dimness of the
night club they shaped an edifice of sound glitter-
ing with notes and swaying to the buffeting of the
drums the way a tall building sways imperceptibly
to the wind when, suddenly, one of the trumpets
sent the edifice toppling with a high, whinnying
chord that seemed to reach beyond sound into silence. It was a signal and the other instruments
quickly followed, the drums exploding into the
erotic beat of a samba, the bass becoming a loud
pulse beneath the shrieking horns—and in the
midst of the hysteria, a voice announced, first in
Portuguese and then in English, "Ladies and gentlemen, the Casa Samba presents *O Grande Caliban e a Pequena Miranda*—The Great Caliban
and the Tiny Miranda!"

The music ended in a taut, expectant silence
and in the darkness a spotlight poured a solid
cone of light onto the stage with such force smoke
seemed to rise from its wide edge and drift out
across the audience. Miranda stood within the
cone of light, alone but for the shadowy forms of

the musicians behind her, as rigid and stiff-faced
as a statue. She was a startlingly tall, long-limbed
woman with white skin that appeared luminous
in the spotlight and blond hair piled like whipped
cream above a face that was just beginning to
slacken with age and was all the more handsome
and arresting because of this. Her brief costume
of sequins and tulle gave off what seemed an iridescent dust each time she breathed, and a smile
was affixed like a stamp to her mouth, disguising
an expression that was, at once, calculating and
grasping—but innocently so, like a child who has
no sense of ownership and claims everything to
be his. Blue eye shadow sprinkled with gold dust
and a pair of dramatic, blue-tinged eyelashes hid
her sullen, bored stare.

She filled the night club with a powerful animal presence, with a decisive, passionless air that
was somehow Germanic. And she was part German, one of those Brazilians from Rio Grande do
Sul who are mixed German, Portuguese, native
Indian and sometimes African. With her the German had triumphed. She was a Brunhild without
her helmet and girdle of mail, without her spear.

There was a rap on the drums and Miranda
clutched one of her buttocks as if she had been
struck there; another rap, louder this time, and
she clutched the other, feigning shock and outrage.

"Hey, lemme in, stupid!" a rough male voice

called in Portuguese behind her, and she whirled like a door that had been kicked open as a dark, diminutive figure burst around her thigh, wearing a scarlet shirt with billowing sleeves and a huge *C* embroidered on the breast like the device of a royal house, a pair of oversized fighter's trunks of the same scarlet which fell past his knees and a prize fighter's high laced shoes.

He was an old man. His hair beneath the matted wig he wore had been gray for years now and his eyes under their crumpled lids were almost opaque with rheum and innocent with age. Yet, as he turned to Miranda with a motion of kicking the door shut, his movements were deft and fluid—his body was still young, it seemed—and as he turned to the audience his face, despite the wrinkles which like fine incisions had drawn his features into an indistinct knot, was still mobile, eloquent, subtle, each muscle beneath the black skin under his absolute control.

Applause greeted him and he assumed the stance of a prize fighter, his body dropping to a wary, menacing crouch, his head ducking and weaving and his tiny fists cocked as he did a dazzling swift dance on his toes. . . . Suddenly he unleashed a flurry of savage jabs, first in the direction of Miranda, who quailed, then at the audience. He pommeled the air and when the knockout blow finally came, it was an uppercut so brilliantly timed, so visually lethal, that those in the audience

who had never seen him before jerked their heads
out of the way of that fist. "Joe Louis, the cham-
pion," he cried, and held up a triumphant right
hand.

He always opened his act this way and the cari-
cature had made him famous and become his trade-
mark. But he had burlesqued at other times in his
long career, and just as effectively, a rustic gazing up at Rio's high buildings of tinted glass and
steel for the first time (this was his favorite since
fifty years ago he had himself come to Rio from a
small jewel-mining town in Minas Gerais), an
American who had just missed his plane (and it
had never mattered that his skin was black or that
he spoke Portuguese, the illusion had held), a matron from the Brazilian upper class whose costume
had begun unraveling during the carnival ball at
Copacabana Palace . . . and others.

He had been Everyman, so much so that it had
become difficult over his thirty-five years in show
business to separate out of the welter of faces he
could assume his face, to tell where O Grande
Caliban ended and he, Heitor Baptista Guimares,
began. He had begun to think about this dimly
ever since the night he had decided to retire—and
to be vaguely disturbed.

Their act was mostly slapstick, with Caliban
using the cowed Miranda as a butt for his bullying
and abuse. And it was this incongruous and contradictory relationship—Caliban's strength, his

bossiness despite his age and shriveled body and
Miranda's weakness, which belied her imposing
height and massive limbs—that was the heart of
their act. It shaped everything they did. When
they sang, as they were doing now, his voice was
an ominous bass rumble beneath her timid so-
prano. They broke into a dance routine and Miranda took little mincing steps while Caliban
spurred his body in a series of impressive leaps
and spins, and forced his legs wide in a split.

It looked effortless, but he felt his outraged
muscles rebel as he repeated the split, his joints
stiffen angrily. He smiled to disguise both his
pain and the disgust he felt for his aging body.
He was suddenly overwhelmed by rage and, as
usual when his anger became unbearable and he
felt helpless, he blamed Miranda. She caught his
angry scowl and paused for an instant that was no
longer than the natural pause between her dance
steps, bewildered, thinking that she had done
something wrong and then understanding (she
knew him far better now that they openly hated
each other), and her own anger streaked across
her eyes even as her smile remained intact.

Halfway through their act Miranda left the
stage and, alone with the spotlight narrowed to
just his face, Caliban spun off a ream of old off-
color jokes and imitations. Everything he did was
flawlessly timed and full of the subtlety and sly-
ness he had perfected over the years, but he was

no longer funny. The audience laughed, but for reasons other than his jokes: the Brazilians out of affection and loyalty, and the tourists, mostly Americans from a Moore-McCormack ship in the harbor, out of a sense of their own well-being and in relief—relief because in the beginning when Caliban's dark face had appeared around Miranda's white thigh they had tensed, momentarily outraged and alarmed until, with smiles that kept slipping out of place, they had reminded each other that this was Brazil after all, where white was never wholly white, no matter how pure it looked. They had begun laughing then in loud, self-conscious gusts, turning to each other for cues and reassurance, whispering, "I don't know why I'm laughing. I don't understand a word of Spanish. Or is this the place where they speak Portuguese?"

Miranda returned for a brief, noisy finale and at the very end she reversed the roles by scooping Caliban up with one hand and marching triumphantly off stage with him kicking, his small arms flailing, high above her head.

"*Senhor* and *Senhoras, O Grande Caliban e a Pequena Miranda!*"

Usually, they took two curtain calls, the first with Miranda still holding the protesting Caliban aloft and the other with Caliban on the ground and in command again, chasing the frightened Miranda across the stage. But, tonight, as soon as they were behind the wing, he ordered her to set him down and when she did, he turned and walked toward his dressing room without a word, his legs stiff with irritability and his set shoulders warning her off.

"Hey, are you crazy, where are you going? The curtain call . . ."

"You take it," he said, without turning. "You think it's your show, so you take it."

She stared after him, helpless and enraged, her eyes a vaporous gray which somehow suggested that her mind was the same gray swirl, and her hair shining like floss in the dimness and dust backstage. Then she bounded after him, an animal about to attack. "Now what did I do wrong?" she shouted against the dwindling sound of the applause.

He turned abruptly and she stopped. "Everything," he said quietly. "You did everything wrong. You were lousy."

"So were you."

"Yes, but only because of you."

"Bastard, whenever something's worrying you or you feel sick, you take it out on me. I swear you're like a woman changing life. Nobody told you to try doing the split out there tonight, straining yourself. You're too old. You should retire. You're finished."

"Shut up."

"Why don't you take out your worries on the

little mamita you have home, your holiest of virgins . . . ?" He walked rapidly away and she cried after him, gesturing furiously, her voice at a scathing pitch, "Yes, go home to mamita, your child bride. And has the holiest of virgins given birth to your little Jesus yet?"

"Pig," he said, and opened the door to his dressing room.

"Children of old men come out crooked." She began to cry, the false eyelashes staining her cheeks blue.

"Barren bitch."

"Runt! Despoiler of little girls."

He slammed the door on her, jarring the mirror on his dressing table so that his reflection wavered out of shape within its somber, mottled depth. He remained near the door, waiting for the mirror to settle and his own anger to subside, aware, as always, of a critical silence in the room. It was a pleasant silence, welcoming him when his performance was good, but mocking and cold—as it was now—when he failed. And he was aware of something else in the room, a subtle disturbance he had sensed there ever since the night, two months ago, when he had decided to retire. He had thought, at first, that the disturbance was due to something out of place within the familiar disorder or to some new object which had been placed there without his knowing it. But after searching and finding nothing, he had come to believe that what he felt was really a disturbance within himself, some worry he could not define which had become dislodged and escaped along with his breath and taken a vague, elusive form outside of him. Each night it awaited him in the cubicle of a dressing room and watched him while he took off his make-up and dressed, mute yet somehow plaintive, like the memory of someone he had known at another time, but whose face he could no longer remember.

Taking off the scarlet shirt, he tossed it among the other costumes littering the room and, sitting at the dressing table, began taking off the make-up, pausing each time the bulb over the mirror flickered out as the music, playing now for the patrons' dancing, jarred the walls. As his face emerged it was clear that it had once been appealing—the way a child's face is—with an abrupt little nose flattened at the tip, a wry mouth and softly molded contours which held dark shadows within their hollows—a face done in miniature over which the black skin had been drawn tight and eyes which held like a banked fire the intensity of the Latin.

He avoided looking at his face now that he was old. Without the make-up it reminded him of a piece of old fruit so shriveled and spotted with decay that there was no certainty as to what it had been originally. Above all, once he removed the make-up, his face was without expression, bland, as though only on stage made up as Caliban in the scarlet shirt and baggy trunks was he at all certain of who he was. Caliban might have become his reality.

So that now, while his hands did the work of his eyes, he gazed absently at his body, imposing on his slack shoulders and on the sunken chest which barely stirred with his breathing the dimmed memory of his body at the height of his fame (he could not remember what it had looked like before becoming Caliban). He had held himself like a military man then, very erect, his small shoulders squared, all of him stretching it seemed toward the height which had been denied him—and this martial stance, so incongruous somehow, had won him the almost hysterical admiration of the crowds. Yet, in the midst of this admiration, he had always felt vaguely like a small animal who had been fitted out in an absurd costume and trained to amuse, some Lilliputian in a kingdom of giants who had to play the jester in order to survive. The world had been scaled without him in mind—and his rage and contempt for it and for those who belonged was always just behind his smile, in the vain, superior lift of his head, in his every gesture.

He pulled on a robe of the same red satin, with a large *C* embroidered on the breast, hiding himself. He flung aside the towel he was using and the light flickered and then flickered again as the door opened and the porter, Henriques, who also served as Caliban's valet, entered with the cup of *café Sinho* he always brought him after the last show.

Caliban watched the reflection take shape behind his in the mirror: the bloated form dressed in a discarded evening jacket with a cummerbund spanning his vast middle, the face a white globule until the beaked nose which absorbed it appeared, and then the fringe of black hair which Henriques kept waved and pomaded. Caliban felt comforted and younger suddenly, so that as Henriques placed the coffee beside him he motioned him to a chair and, turning, said, his voice loud and casual but strained:

"Henriques, we are in business, old man. Or better out of business. The signs are finished. I saw them today. And they are good. Very bold. They used my red and it hits the eye like one of Caliban's uppercuts"—his fist cut through the air and, although Henriques laughed and nodded, no smile stirred within his old eyes.

"And, thank God, they got the *C* in Caliban right. I was worried about that because they got it all wrong on the posters they made for my tour last year. But it pleased me the way they did the *C* this time. Very large and sweeping. Up at the top it says, 'O Grande Caliban retiring,' in big print to catch the eye, with the *C* coming at you like a fist, then below that 'Brazil's greatest and most beloved comedian leaving the stage after

thirty-five years,' and at the bottom, 'See him perform for the last times this month at the Casa
Samba.' That's all. And enough, I think. It is
more dramatic that way. . . ."

"And when will they be put on display, Senhor
Caliban?" Henriques asked with elaborate cour-
tesy.

"The day after tomorrow. The posters will go
up all over the city, but the big signs only downtown and in Copacabana. There'll be announcements in all the papers of course—a full-page ad
which will run for a week, and on radio and tele-
vision."

"I have a confession, senhor," Henriques said,
his voice edging in beside Caliban's, which had
grown louder, filling the room. "I personally did
not believe it. You know, senhor, how you sometimes talk about retiring but . . . well, you
know. But now with the signs and the announcements . . ."

"The talk has ended, Henriques. Two more
weeks. The signs are ready, old man!" He
shouted as though informing someone beyond the
room and held up two fingers the color and shape
of dried figs. "Two weeks from tonight Caliban
does his last boxing match. That night will mark
my anniversary. Thirty-five years ago that same
night I won the amateur contest at the Teatro
Municipal. Do you remember the old Teatro
Municipal? There's a clinic there now for the chil-

dren of the poor. The night I won, the producer, Julio Baretos, right away booked me in his regular show and christened me O Grande Caliban. After that . . ." His gesture summed up the success which had followed that night.

"And what is your real name, Senhor Caliban?" Henriques said.

Caliban paused, surprised for the moment, and then quickly said, "Guimares. Heitor Guimares. Heitor Baptista Guimares." He gave an embarrassed laugh. "I haven't used it for so long I had to stop and think."

"Perhaps you will begin using it now that you are retiring."

"Of course," he said, and sat back, his smile and gesture dying, his eyes becoming troubled again under their crumpled lids. He quickly drank the *café Sinho* and, as his glance met Henriques' over the cup, he gave a shapeless smile. "Of course," he repeated loudly, even as his gaze wandered over the costumes hung like the bright skins of imaginary animals on the walls, over the trunks containing his juggling and magician equipment. His eyes lingered on each object, possessing it. He tied the scarlet robe more securely around him.

"You are wise to retire," Henriques said quietly. "After all, you are not that old yet and you have a new life ahead what with a young wife and a child soon."

"Of course," Caliban murmured, and for a moment could not remember what his wife looked like.

"How many your age have that? Look at me. I haven't been able to have a woman for years now. And children? All my children have forgotten me. And you have money, Senhor Caliban, while we who are old and without must keep dragging around a dead carcass, breathing death over everybody, working till our end. . . ." Henriques stirred heavily in the chair, looking, with the costumes draped behind him and the cummerbund girding his middle, like some old, sated regent.

"Yes," he said, and followed Caliban's stare into space. "You are retiring at the right time, senhor, and with dignity. Putting up the signs all over the city shows style. You are saying good-by to Rio in the proper way, which is only right, since it was here that you became famous. Rio made you, after all."

"Of course."

"Now once a year during carnival you will perform before the President at Copacabana Palace Hotel and all of Rio will weep remembering your greatness. . . ."

Caliban restrained him with a gesture and in the silence his dark skin seemed to grow ashen as if inside some abstract terror had cramped his heart. "What to do, Henriques," he said, and shrugged. "I am an old man. Did you see me tonight? The last show especially? I could hardly

move. I forgot lines so that the jokes didn't make
sense. I was all right in the beginning, but once I
gave the knockout punch I was through. That
punch took all my strength. I feel it here," he
touched his right shoulder, his chest. "Oh, I know
I could go on working at the Casa Samba for a
while longer, I am an institution here, but I don't
love it any more. I don't feel the crowd. And then
that pig Miranda has gotten so lousy."

"Did you have her name put on the signs?"

"To hell with her. No," he shouted, swept suddenly by the same anger he had felt on stage. He
jumped up and began dressing under Henriques'
somnolent eye, wondering at the intensity of his
anger, knowing remotely that it reached beyond
Miranda to something greater.

"But haven't you told her?"

"I told her. I even told her about the signs. But
like you she didn't believe me. She just laughed.
The pig," he cried suddenly, and the light flickered. "Did you hear her cursing me just now, and
cursing my wife and my unborn child. She has
become crazy this past year. All because I married." Suddenly, facing the door, he shouted, "It's
my business that I married, pig, not yours. And
if I chose to marry a child of twenty-five, it is my
business still."

He waited, quivering, as though expecting Miranda to burst into the room. Then, turning again
to Henriques, he said, "You would not believe it,

Henriques, but I still give her everything she
wants even though I married. Last month she saw
one of those fancy circular beds in a magazine
from Hollywood and I had one custom made for
her. A while back, she took out all the light fixtures
and put in chandeliers, even in the kitchen, so that
her place looks like the grand ballroom of the
Copacabana Palace Hotel. I bought the chandeliers for her, of course, as I have bought nearly
everything she has—while she has been saving her
money all these years. And even though I married
I still go and spend part of the evening with her
before we come to the club. . . . So she com-
plains I will have nothing to do with her any more.
But after all, Henriques, I am an old man and I
have a young wife. Besides it was always a little
grotesque with her. . . ."

"They say it's never good to keep a woman
around once you're finished with her."

"I should have kicked her out, yes—and long
ago. She was never any good for me or for the act.
From the very beginning she tried to take over
both of us. And I only included her in the act for
effect. She wasn't supposed to do anything more
than stand there like a mannequin. But she kept
insisting—she would wake me at night begging me
to let her do more. And so . . ." He motioned
hopelessly and sat down.

"I should have never taken up with her." Then
he said softly, "But she was a weakness with me

in the beginning." He gave Henriques an
oblique, almost apologetic glance. "And what I
said just now was not true. She was good for me
in the beginning—and we were good together. We
were the same, you see. Me, as I am—" and with
a gesture he offered Henriques his shrunken
body—"and she, so tall, and she was skinny then.
They were laughing at her the first time I saw her
in a show at the Miramar almost fifteen years ago
now. She couldn't dance. She couldn't sing. She
hadn't bleached her hair yet and she looked lousy.
. . . I understood what it was for her being so
tall—" His voice dropped, becoming entangled
with the memory. "And she was good for the act
in the beginning. She had imagination and the
comic touch. She was the one who thought up the
prize-fighter routine, which is still the most famous. But then something went wrong with her,
Henriques, and she began doing everything
wrong. I've been carrying her for years now. Perhaps I would have had another five, ten years
left, if not for her. She has become a bane. She has
used me till I'm dry, the pig!"

"But what of her now?"

Caliban, dressed in an expensive mohair suit
with a white handkerchief embroidered with a red
C in the breast pocket, patent-leather shoes with
built-up heels and diamond cuff links glinting in
turn with the many rings he wore, turned sharply
toward the door as if to rush from the room and

the question. "What of her? That's not my worry.
The day those signs go up is the day I finish with
her, the parasite. Let her spend some of the money
she sits on. She has talked for years about doing
her own act. Now she'll have a chance to do it."

"But does she have the talent for that?"

"No, and she knows it. Do you think she would
have stayed with me all this time if she had, Henriques? Not Miranda."

"Well, she will find someone to keep her. She is
like Rio. There will always be somebody to admire
her." Henriques heaved up from the chair, and,
as his unwieldy bulk filled the small room, the
dusk whirred up like frightened birds and settled
further away. He began picking up Caliban's
clothes.

"Yes," Caliban said thoughtfully, "she will find
somebody to use, the bitch. For a while anyway."
He hurried to the door, eager to escape the room
which had suddenly become crowded with the
image of Miranda and hot from his anger. As he
opened it, he sensed the vague, illusory form of his
fear rush past him like a draft and lead him
through the clutter backstage, out the back door
and across the denuded yard to the entrance,
where the neon lights pulsed the name CASA SAMBA
into the night and a large sign at the door announced the nightly appearance of O Grande
Caliban.

The club was closing; the last of the crowd

clustered under the awning while the doorman called up the taxis. Beyond the radius of neon lights the night itself was a vast awning under which the city slept, exhausted from its nightly revelry, its few remaining lights like dull reflections of the stars. Its mountains, like so many dark breasts thrusting into the sky, gave height and prominence and solidity to the night.

The Casa Samba had been built on the sloping street leading to the *Pão de Açúcar* and as Caliban walked toward his car he was aware, as if for the first time, of the mountain's high, solid cone, black against the lesser blackness of the sky, benevolent, rising protectively over the sleeping city. He could make out the cable line of the aerial railway looped in a slender thread between *Pão de Açúcar* and its satellite, Mount Urca. What had been for years just another detail in the familiar frieze that was Rio was suddenly separate and distinct, restored. . . . He paused beside his car, hoping (but unaware of the hope) that a part of himself which he had long since ceased to see might emerge into consciousness as the mountain had emerged, thinking (and he was aware of this) that there might be a wind the day after tomorrow when the signs announcing his retirement went up, a wind strong enough to tear them down before they could be read and whip them out to sea. He was half smiling, his worn eyelids closing with pleasure at the thought, when a taxi with a group of Americans from the night club stopped and one of them called to him in English, "Say, do you speak English?"

He turned, annoyed. The man's voice, the harsh, unmelodic, almost guttural English he spoke, his pale face floating in the darkness seemed to snatch his pleasure, to declare that there would be no wind the day after tomorrow and the signs would remain. As the taxi's headlights singled him out, he felt as if he had been caught on stage without the armor of his scarlet shirt and loose trunks—suddenly defenseless, shorter than his five feet, insignificant. He quickly assumed his martial pose.

"I speak some little English," he said stiffly.

"Well, then maybe you can explain to our driver here—" and the driver protested in Portuguese to Caliban that he had understood them and could speak English—"that we want to go someplace else, not back to the hotel, but to another night club. Are there any that stay open all night? Do you understand what I'm saying? Some place where we can dance."

Without answering, Caliban turned and told the driver where to take them. Then he said in English, "He will take you to a place."

"Thanks. Say, aren't you the comedian from the club? What's your name again?"

He wanted to fling the full title—O Grande Caliban—in the man's face and walk away, but he could not even say Caliban. For some reason he felt suddenly divested of that title and its distinction, no longer entitled to use it.

The man was whispering to the others in the car. "What was his name again? You know, the old guy telling the jokes. With the blonde."

"The name is Heitor Guimares," Caliban said suddenly.

"No, I mean your stage name."

"Hey, wait, I remember," someone in the car called. "It was from Shakespeare. Caliban . . ."

"Heitor Baptista Guimares," he cried, his voice loud and severe, addressed not only to them but to the mountain and the night. Turning, he walked to his car.

He did not drive away but remained perched like a small, ruffled bird on the cushions he used to raise the driver's seat, his rings winking angrily in the dimness as he watched the taillights of the taxi define the slope as it sped down, trying to order his breathing, which had suddenly become a conscious and complex act. The taillights vanished and with them the momentary annoyance he had felt with the tourists. He was alone then, with only the vague form of his anxiety (and he had never felt such loneliness) and the unfamiliar name echoing in his mind.

"Heitor Guimares," he said slowly. "Heitor Guimares." But although he repeated it until his tongue was heavy, it had no reality. It was the name of a stranger who had lived at another time.

By the time Caliban reached the modern house of glass walls and stone he had built in a suburb near Corcovado, the mountain of Christ, a thin, opalescent dawn had nudged aside the darkness, and, as he walked hesitantly across the patio, through the living room, down the hall to the bedrooms, the sound of his raised heels on the tiles was like the failing pulse of the dying night.

He paused at the opened door of the master bedroom. He could not hear his wife's breathing but he could see it in the small, steady flame of the candle before the Madonna in the niche near the bed. In the faint light he made out her stomach, like a low hill on the wide plain of the bed, and the dark outline of her face framed by the pillows. He did not have to see that face to know its mildness and repose. The first time he had met her on the tour last year which had taken him through the small town in Minas Gerais where he had been born (she was the granddaughter of a distant cousin of his and it had been easy to arrange the marriage), he had almost, instinctively, crossed himself. She had looked like a Madonna painted black. He had wanted to confess to her as to a priest, seeing her that first time. He would have confessed now if he could have named his fear— whispering to her while she slept. And she would have, blindly in her sleep, curved her body to receive him, nesting him within the warm hollow of

her back as if he were the child she bore. He hesitated though, feeling, oddly, that he was no longer
entitled to her comfort, just as he was no longer
entitled to use the name Caliban.

He closed the door and went to the small room at
the end of the hall which he used as a den and
stretched out on the cot there without undressing.
As always when he was troubled, he slept quickly
and his dream was that he was caught in a mine
shaft without a lantern to light his way.

As quickly, light rushed at him from one end of
the shaft and he awoke to the afternoon sun which
had invaded the room. Like a reveler the sunlight
did a sprightly dance on the framed photographs
on the walls (they were all of Caliban, one with
the President of Brazil during the carnival of
1946 and another with Carmen Miranda the year
before she died), on the mementoes and awards
on top of the desk; it leaped across the floor and
landed in the arms of his wife as she opened the
door.

She did not enter the room but stood, like a peti-
tioner, in the doorway, holding a cup of coffee as
though it was an offering. She had already been to
Mass, yet a thin haze from her long sleep filmed
her eyes; her body, Caliban knew, would still be
warm and pliant from the bed. He felt neither
pleasure nor passion at the thought, though—and
as if she understood this and blamed herself, she
bowed her head.

"Caliban . . ." she said finally, and hesitated. Then: "You have slept in all your clothes and in your rings."

"It's nothing," he said, and sat up, waving her off as she started forward to help him. "I was tired last night, that's all."

His body felt strange: sore as though he had been beaten while he slept, constricted by the clothes which seemed to have shrunk overnight. The taste of the name he had spoken aloud in the car was still in his mouth. "Let me have the coffee," he said.

The coffee was the color and texture of his sleep and he drank it quickly, wishing that it was a potion which would bring on that sleep again. "Is there a wind today?"

"Only at the top of the road, near the church." And she quickly added, "But I wore a coat."

His thought had been of the signs, not of her, and, ashamed suddenly, he said in the paternal, indulgent tone he used with her, "Tell me, Clara, how would you like to live somewhere else for a while? Somewhere in Minas again perhaps . . ."

She could not disguise her reluctance. "Back to Minas? But what of your work?"

"You let me worry about that, little Clara."

"And this house?"

"Sell it and build a bigger one there."

"Yes, of course. But then Rio is nice too. I mean there is carnival here and . . ."

"We will come down for carnival each year."

"Of course. Then there is the child. It would be nice if it were born in Rio. Perhaps after the child we could return to Minas. . . ."

"No, I don't want a child of mine to be born in Rio and be called a *Carioca*."

"Yes, Caliban."

"Say Heitor," he said sharply, startling her.

"Heitor?" She frowned.

"Don't you know my real name?"

"Of course."

"Well, then, you can begin using it."

She would have asked why (he could see the question stir within the haze), but she was not bold enough.

For the first time her timidity annoyed him and he leaped up, his movement so abrupt that she drew back. "Tell me," he said, appealing to her suddenly, "did your mother ever speak about me? Or your grandmother? Did they ever talk about me as a young man? About Heitor?"

"Of course."

"What did they say I was like?"

She was silent for so long he repeated the question, his voice high and urgent. "What did they say?"

"I know they used to talk about how big a success you were . . ." she said hesitantly.

"As a young man, I said. Before I came to Rio. I was different then. . . ."

"I know they used to talk, but I can't remember all that they said. I only know that when you were famous they always looked for your name in the papers."

He sat down on the edge of the cot, showing his disgust with her by a limp wave and feeling unreasonably that she had failed him. It was as if he had married her hoping that she would bring, like a dowry, the stories and memories of him as a young man, as Heitor, only to discover that he had been cheated.

"Heitor Guimares . . . Senhora Guimares," she was murmuring, touching herself and smiling abstractly.

"What are you laughing about? You don't like the name?"

"No, it's just that until I get used to it I will keep looking for someone else when I say it because I'm so used to you being Caliban."

It was not clear whether he hurled the cup at her or at the floor, but it missed her and, as it broke on the tiles, the sunlight scuttled from the room and the spilled coffee spread in a dark stain between them. "And who will you be looking for?" His shout was strident with the same abstract rage of the night before. "Who? Tell me. Some boy your age perhaps? Some tall, handsome boy, eh, some *Carioca* who will dance with you in the streets during carnival and jounce you on my bed behind my back? Is he the one you will be looking for?"

She said nothing. She had uttered a muted cry when the cup broke, but now, as he leaped up again, she calmly placed her hands over her swollen stomach, protecting it from the violence of his movement and, as he shouted, her fat child's fingers spread wider, deflecting the sound.

"Tell me!" he charged her. "Who is this person you will be looking for when you call my name?"

She remained as silent and resigned as the Virgin in their bedroom, her head bent in submission, her hands guarding the stomach.

Her silence was a defense he could not shake and as he stood there, menacing her with his shouts, he felt his anger rebound from the thick, invisible wall of silence which shielded her and flail him. He was the victim of his own rage, and bruised, beaten, he rushed from the room, from her, his heels clattering like small hoofs on the tile.

"Caliban!" He heard her cry over the sound of the motor as he started the car, and then a snatch of words as he drove off: "You have not changed your clothes."

He realized this when he was some distance from the house and had calmed a little. And the feel of the stale, sodden clothes recalled the time when he had first come to Rio and had had to wear secondhand clothes that were invariably too large for him and shiny from long wear and smelling always of the former owners. That had been the time, of course, when he had been only Heitor

Guimares and people calling him by that name had not looked for anyone else, nor had he felt strange saying it. He tried to restore those years in his mind, but the memories were without form or coherence. They filtered down at random, blown like dust through his mind, and as he reached out to snatch them—desperate suddenly to recapture that time and that self—they eluded his fingers.

One memory paused though: he saw a street, the Rua Gloria, and the restaurant where he had worked until he had won the contest at the Teatro Municipal. The pattern of the tile floor over which he had swung the mop three times a day, the tables—slabs of cheap white marble upon which he had placed the food—were suddenly clear. He had left a part of himself there. Suddenly he brought his foot down on the accelerator, standing up and gripping the steering wheel to give himself leverage, and the big car bounded forward, bearing him to the city and the Rua Gloria.

As the car swept down the mountain roads, the sea appeared, vast and benign, mirroring the sky's paleness and breaking the sun's image into fragments, then the bays—sure, graceful curves, forming an arabesque design with the hills between—and finally the city itself—white, opulent, languorous under the sun's caress, taking its afternoon rest now in preparation for the night.

The Rua Gloria was in the old section of Rio and Caliban found it easily, recognizing the house on the corner with its Moorish-style balcony and checker-pane windows. The house was a ruin but somehow it promised that he would find the restaurant at the other end of the street. Parking the car, he started down, eager suddenly. Instinctively, as if the years had not passed, his legs made the slight adjustment to the sloping street and his feet sought out the old holes in the pavement; halfway down he passed the boys' school and his head turned automatically, expecting the boys in the yard to wave and shout, "*Ohlá*, Senhor Heitor, when are you going to stop growing?"

There were boys in the yard now, playing soccer in the eddying dust, and they looked no different from those he had known. But they did not wave, and, although they shouted and rushed out the gate when he passed, it was only because he was a stranger. They pointed to his mohair suit, his shoes with the raised heels, his rings dancing in the sunlight, whispering among themselves. And then one of them cried, "O Grande Caliban," and, with that abruptness which Caliban had perfected, dropped to a fighter's crouch. The others took up his cry and the name O Grande Caliban rose in a piercing chorale.

They trailed him, trumpeting the name, a scuffling retinue in their school uniforms. Caliban stiffened each time they tossed his name into the

air like a football, but he welcomed them. They
were a solid wall between him and the apprehensiveness which trailed him. Because of them he
was certain that he would find the restaurant intact, like the setting of a play which had not been
dismantled.

And it was there, but unrecognizable save
for the glazed tiles in the entrance way which
were all broken now and the stone doorsill in
which the old groove had been worn deeper. Where
the awning had been, a huge sign said BEBE COCA-
COLA and below that, on the modern glass front,
was the new name of the restaurant: O RESTAU-
RANTE GRANDE CALIBAN.

The boys crowded behind him, pressing him inside, and he saw that the tile floor whose every
imperfection he could have traced in the dark had
been covered in bright linoleum; chrome chairs
and tables had replaced the marble tables and
wire-back chairs, while booths covered in simulated leather lined one wall. The air smelled of
stale coffee and as Caliban, jarred by the sight of
faded newspaper photographs of himself crowding
the walls and a garish oil painting of him in the
scarlet shirt hanging over the bar, placed his hand
on a table to steady himself, a fly there stirred its
wings but did not move.

The only occupant was a man—the waiter or
owner perhaps—half-asleep at the bar, his stout

haunches overlapping the stool. He stirred into
wakefulness now with the same blind, stubborn
movement as the fly. He was a *sarará* with an
abundance of sandy hair curling out of the sweat-
shirt he wore, fair skin pitted from smallpox and
small, agate-colored eyes set within morose features. He turned, querulous with sleep, and missing Caliban, who was, after all, no taller than most
of the boys, he shouted, "Get out of here, you
little bandits, before you let in the flies."

"We come with Caliban," they hurled at him,
"O Grande Caliban."

The man started suspiciously and peered, his
head lowered as though he was about to charge,
through the fog of sleep. As he spotted Caliban
his agate-colored eyes glittered like one of Caliban's rings, and an awed smile groped its
way around his mouth. "Senhor Caliban . . .?"
he whispered, and slipped from the stool into a
bow so fluid and perfect it looked rehearsed.

"Senhor Caliban, it is a great honor. . . ."
With a proud wave he presented Caliban with the
large portrait over the bar, the photographs, the
chrome chairs and the linoleum. "Please . . ."
He motioned him to a booth, then to a table.

Caliban would have turned and left if the boys
had not been behind him, barring his way. He
wanted to escape, for the restaurant had profaned
his past with chrome and simulated leather, and

the portrait, the faded photographs, his name on the window had effaced the Heitor Guimares who had wielded the mop over the tiles.

"Who put up those pictures?" he asked sharply.

The man's smile faltered and he said, puzzled, "I found them here when I bought the place, Senhor Caliban, all except the portrait. I did that. I am something of a painter—an artist like yourself, Senhor Caliban. I did it in your honor. . . ." He gave the supple bow again.

"Who owned the place before you?"

"A man named DaCruz. He had many debts so I got it cheap . . ."

"Did he put them up?"

"No, I think it was his great-uncle, old Nacimento, the one, Senhor Caliban, who must have owned the restaurant when you worked here. Perhaps you've forgotten him?"

"Yes, I had forgotten," Caliban said, and paused, trying to summon Nacimento's face from the blurred assortment of faces in his mind. "Is he still alive?"

"He was the last time I heard, Senhor Caliban, but he is very sick because of course he is so old. And he has nothing now, I hear, and lives in the *favelas*."

"Which one?"

"The one above Copacabana . . . Senhor Caliban, a *café Sinho* perhaps?"

But Caliban had already turned and with an abrupt wave scattered the boys out of his way.

"A *café Sinho*, at least!" The man shouted from the doorway over the heads of the boys, but Caliban, his small back slanted forward, was already rushing up the street, his patent-leather shoes flashing in the sunlight.

Later, as Caliban climbed the first slope leading to the *favela*, his shoes became covered with red dust and clay. He could see just above him the beginning of the slums—a vast, squalid rookery for the poor of Rio clinging to the hill above Copacabana, a nest of shacks built with the refuse of the city: the discarded crates and boxes, bits of galvanized iron and tin, old worm-eaten boards and shingles—and all of this piled in confused, listing tiers along the hillside, the wood bleached gray by the sun. The *favela* was another city above Rio which boldly tapped its electricity from below—so that at night the hills were strewn with lights—and repulsed the government's efforts to remove it. It was an affront—for that squalor rising above Rio implied that Rio herself was only a pretense; it was a threat—for it seemed that at any moment the *favela* would collapse and hurtle down, burying the city below.

Caliban had long ago ceased to see the *favelas*. He would glance up at the hills occasionally to watch them shift miraculously as the shadows moving across them shifted, but his eye passed quickly over the ugliness there: it was too much a reminder of what he had known. Now the *favela* claimed his eye. It seemed to rush down at him, bringing with it a sure and violent death—and he remembered the stories of strangers who had ventured into the *favelas* and had either disappeared or been found garroted the next day at the foot of the hill.

In pursuing the old man, it was as if, suddenly, he was pursuing his own death. And because he was exhausted, the thought of that death was almost pleasurable. He imagined the thronged cathedral, the crowds standing a thousand deep outside, the city hung in crape; he heard the priest intoning his name—and at the thought that perhaps no one would recognize the name Heitor Guimares, he stumbled and nearly fell.

The children of the *favela* appeared, slipping quietly down amid the scrub which lined the path, some of them balancing gallon tins of water on their heads or smaller children on their hips. They seemed born of the dust which covered them, like small, tough plants sprung from the worn soil, and their flat, incurious eyes seemed to mirror the defeated lives they had yet to live.

They watched him climb without comment, recognizing that he was a stranger from the city below who brought with him the trappings of that world: the flashing rings and stylish clothes. Their empty stares seemed to push him up the hill toward some final discovery.

Caliban could not look at them, and said, his eyes averted, "*Ohlá*, can any of you tell me where to find Nacimento, the old man?"

Their answer was a stolid silence and he called down the line, addressing each one in turn: "Do you know him? Which is his house? Do you know who I'm talking about?" Finally he cried, his voice strained thin by the dust and his exertion, "Do you know him; he is an old friend!"

"His house is the one there," a boy said finally, pointing. "The one beside the tree without a head."

Caliban saw the tree, a dead palm without its headdress of fronds, starting out of the ground like a derisive finger, and then the house beside it, a makeshift of old boards and tin and dried fronds. It looked untenanted: Nacimento might have died and left the house as a monument. Caliban turned to the children, the fear dropping like a weight inside him.

"He's there," the boy said. "He doesn't like the sun."

And suddenly Caliban remembered Nacimento sending him to roll down the restaurant awning against the sun each afternoon. The warped door he pushed open now seemed to declare the age of the man inside and, as he entered the room, shutting out the glare behind him, it was as if the night was in hiding there, waiting for the sun to set before it rushed out and, charging down the hill, lay siege to the city.

"Nacimento . . ." he called softly. He could not see the old man but he heard his breathing—a thin *râle* like the fluting of an instrument Nacimento played to ease his loneliness. Presently Caliban made out a table because of a white cup there, then a cot whose legs had been painted white and finally the dark form of the old man.

He was seated before the boarded-up window, facing it as though it was open, and he was watching the sun arching down the sky or the children waiting around the dead palm for Caliban to emerge.

"Nacimento," Caliban said, and knew that the old man was blind. "Senhor Nacimento."

"Is there someone?" the old man asked uncertainly, as though he could no longer distinguish between those voices which probably filled his fantasies sitting there alone and those that were real. He did not turn from the window.

"Yes, it is Heitor Guimares."

"Who is the person?" The old man said formally, turning now.

"Heitor."

"Heitor?"

"Yes, from the restaurant years ago. You remember. He . . . I used to be the waiter. . . ."

"Heitor . . ." the old man said slowly, as

though searching for the face to which the name belonged.

Hopeful, Caliban drew closer. He could see Nacimento's eyes now, two yellow smears in the dimness which reflected nothing and the face wincing, it seemed, in unrelieved pain.

"Yes, Heitor," Caliban said coaxingly. "You used to call me Little Heitor from Minas. You remember. . . ."

"I know no Heitor," the old man said sorrowfully, and then, starting apprehensively, he cried, "Is the door closed? The sun ruins everything."

Caliban's voice rose, tremulous and insistent. "But of course you remember. After all, every day you used to tell me the same thing—to close the door, to roll down the awning against the sun. It was I—Heitor Guimares—who would sometimes tell a few jokes at night to keep the customers drinking. But then, you must remember because it was you, after all, who made me enter the amateur contest at the Teatro Municipal. You even went with me that night and gave me a shirt to wear with ruffles down the front like a movie star. The Teatro Municipal!" he shouted as the old man shook his head confusedly. "We wept on each other's shoulder when they told me I had won and put me in the regular show with the name of Caliban. . . ."

"O Grande Caliban," the old man said severely.

"Yes, but I was Heitor Guimares when I worked for you, not Caliban."

"O Grande Caliban. He was the best they ever had at the Teatro Municipal. I told him he would win and he was the best. . . ."

"But I was Heitor then!"

"I know no Heitor," Nacimento cried piteously, and turned to the boarded-up window, reaching up as though he would open it and call for help. "I know no Heitor. . . ."

Caliban believed him. It was no use. The old man, he understood, going suddenly limp, had retained only a few things: his fear of the sun, the name O Grande Caliban, a moment of success in a crowded theater in which he had shared. That was all. The rest had been stripped away in preparation for his death which, in a way, had already begun. Caliban smelled its stench in the room suddenly and wanted to flee as he had fled the restaurant earlier. Groping toward the door, he jarred against the table and the cup there fell and broke. The old man whimpered at the sound and Caliban remembered his wife's muted outcry that morning over the other cup he had broken. The day seemed to be closing in on him, squeezing his life from him, and his panic was like a stitch in his side as he rushed out, forgetting to close the door behind him.

The night might have escaped through the open door and followed him down the hill, for as he sat in his car, crumpled with exhaustion, knowing that his search had been futile and he could do nothing now but go to Miranda as he did each evening at this time, he saw the first of the dusk surge across the hill in a dark, purposeful wave, drowning out the *favela*, and then charge down the slopes, deepening into night as it came.

The city, in quick defense, turned on her lights, and as Caliban drove out of the tunnel onto the road which followed the wide arc of Copacabana Bay he saw the lights go on in the apartment buildings and hotels piled like white angular cliffs against the black hills. Seen from a distance those lighted windows resembled very large, fine diamonds, an iridescent amber now in the last of the sunlight, which would turn to a fiery yellow once the darkness settled. Rio—still warm from the sun, murmurous with the cadence of the sea, bejeweled with lights—was readying herself for the nightly carousal, waiting for the wind to summon her lovers.

Caliban had been one of her lovers, but as he drove through her midst, he felt her indifference to his confusion, to his sense of a loss which remained nameless; moreover, he suspected that she had even been indifferent to his success. "After all Rio has made you," Henriques had said, but he had not added that she would quickly choose another jester to her court once he was gone. Caliban hated the city suddenly—and as that hate became unbearable he shifted its weight onto Miranda. He accused her. Hadn't Henriques said that she and Rio were the same? He brought his foot down on the accelerator and the car leaped forward like a startled horse, leaving black streaks on the road.

Oddly enough, Miranda's apartment, in a new building at the end of Copacabana, reflected the city. The great squares of black and white tile in the foyer suggested not only the stark white buildings reared against the dark hills and the sidewalks of Copacabana—a painstaking mosaic of small black and white stones, but the faces of the *Cariocas* themselves—endless combinations of black and white. The green rug in the living room could have been a swatch cut from one of the hills, while the other furnishings there—elaborate period pieces of an ivory finish, marble tables cluttered with figurines, sofas of pale silk and down, white drapes and gilt-edged mirrors—repeated the opulence, self-indulgence, the lavish whiteness of the city. And the chandeliers with their fiery crystal spears, which rustled like frosted leaves as Caliban slammed the door, caught the brilliance of Rio at night.

For the first time Caliban was aware of how the room expressed the city, and of himself, reflected in one of the mirrors, in relation to it. He was like a house pet, a tiny dog, who lent the room an amusing touch but had no real place there. The pale walls and ivory furniture, the abundance of white throughout stripped him of importance, denied him all significance. He felt like whimpering as the old man, Nacimento, had whimpered when the cup broke—and he must have unknowingly, for Miranda suddenly called from the adjoining bedroom, "What in the hell are you muttering to yourself about out there?"

He turned and through the half-opened door saw her enthroned amid a tumble of pink satin cushions on the circular bed he had bought her, while her maid massaged her feet in a basin of scented water—the girl's black hands wavering out of shape under the water. Miranda had already dressed her hair for the night club—the stiff froth of blond curls piled high above her white brow—and applied her make-up (she had spent the afternoon at it, Caliban knew), but her body beneath the sheer pink dressing gown was still bare, the tops of the breasts a darker pink than the gown. Knowing how slack those breasts had become, Caliban felt repelled, weary and then angry again; he understood suddenly that her refusal ever to leave him and marry, to have children and use those ample breasts, was, simply, her desire to remain the child herself—willful, dependent, indulged—and that she had used him to this end, just as she would use someone else now that she had exhausted him.

As always when he was truly angry, he became calm, and in that calm he could always feel his nerves, the muscles of his abrupt little arms and legs, his heart, quietly marshaling their force for the inevitable outburst. He came and stood in the doorway, very still, the only exterior signs of his anger a tightness around his mouth, a slight tension to his wide nose and a chill light within his even gaze.

Without looking up from polishing her nails, Miranda said querulously, "You come in late slamming my doors and then you stand outside talking to yourself. Where have you been all day anyway? People have been calling here looking for you after they called your house and that stupid child you married said she didn't know where you had gone."

She glanced up, still sullen and truculent from their quarrel the night before—and stiffened. Her maid felt her foot go taut and turned, puzzled.

"Go home, Luiz," he said quietly.

Miranda screamed, the sound jarring the bottle of nail polish from her hand and it spilled, staining the pink covers red. "No, Luiz . . ." She reached toward the girl. "Wait, Luiz . . ."

"Go home, Luiz," he repeated.

The girl stood up then as though jerked to her feet and, holding the basin of water, looked from him to Miranda for a single distraught moment and then broke for the door, the water sloshing on the rug. As she passed him, Caliban said gently,

"Good night, Luiz," and closed the door behind her.

"*Luiz!*"

Caliban came and sat across the bed from her and deliberately placed his trouser leg with the red dust and clay from the *favela* against the pink coverlet.

Miranda stared at the leg, her gray eyes dull with hysteria and disbelief, at the nail polish streaked like fresh blood on the bedclothes and her hands, at the trail of water the maid had left on the rug and then across to the closed door. Her skin blanched with terror and her scream convulsed the air again, higher this time, so that the chandelier over her bed swayed anxiously. And still screaming, cursing incoherently, she frantically began drawing up the sheet around her.

"Tell me," Caliban said evenly, "do you know a Heitor Guimares?"

She did not hear him at first and he waited until her scream broke off and then repeated in the same quiet tone, "I asked you if you know somebody named Heitor Guimares?"

"Who?" The word was uttered at the same high pitch as her scream.

"Heitor Guimares."

"Heitor who . . . ? Guimares. No. Who is that? I don't know anybody by that name. Guimares . . . ?" Wary, suspicious, she said after a

pause, "Why do you ask?" and then emboldened
by his silence, shouted, "What is this? Why do
you come asking me about someone I don't know.
Who's this Heitor Guimares anyway? Why do you
come in here looking as if you slept in the sewers
and muttering to yourself, scaring me, scaring my
maid, slamming my doors and ruining my bed
with your dirt. Oh, God, what's wrong now? It's
going to be hell tonight. You'll do everything
wrong in the show and blame me. You're old!"
she screamed, and started up in the bed. "And losing your mind. You should retire. Go back to
Minas, peasant. . . . And that little bitch, she's
fired. I won't pay her a cent for ruining the rug.
Everything ruined . . ." she said tragically,
and paused, looking tearfully down at the spilled
nail polish on her hands, quiet for the moment,
and then her head snapped up. "Who is this
Heitor Guimares now? I lie here alone all day, all
night, alone, always alone, and then you come in
here accusing me of someone I don't know. Bastard! Suppose I did know someone by that name.
It would be my business. You don't own me. I'm
not your scared little mamita. Heitor Guimares!
Who is he? Somebody has been feeding you lies."

"I am Heitor Guimares."

She stared at him, the rest of what she had to
say lying dead on her lips and the wildness still in
her eyes. Then her bewilderment collapsed into a
laugh that was as shrill, in relief, as her scream

had been. The sheet she was holding around her dropped and her arm shot out, stiff with scorn. "You? No, senhor, you are Caliban. O Grande Caliban!" And leaping from the bed, her great breasts swinging, she dropped to his familiar fighter's crouch, her fists cocked menacingly and her smile confirming what the others—his wife that morning, the boys on the Rua Gloria chanting behind him, the man in the restaurant that had been made into a shrine, and, finally, the old man, Nacimento—had all insisted was true, and what he, and certainly Miranda, had really known all along: simply, that Caliban had become his only reality and anything else he might have been was lost. The image Miranda had created for him was all he had now and once that was taken—as it would be tomorrow when the signs announcing his retirement went up—he would be left without a self.

Miranda did not see him pick up the small boudoir chair, for her head was lowered over her fists and she was doing the little shuffling fighter's dance he had made famous. But as the chair cut the air above her, her head snapped up, her hand started up and she watched its flight with the mocking smile her shock and stupefaction had fixed on her face. She tried to move but could not. It was too late anyway; the chair smashed into the low-hanging chandelier and brought it down in a roar of shattered crystal onto the bed—and in the light from the small lamps along the walls the bed seemed to explode in a thick, mushrooming cloud of pink dust.

Caliban's destruction of the apartment was swift and complete. It was as if the illusion of strength he had created on stage for so long had been finally given to him. While Miranda stood transfixed, a dazed horror spreading like a patina over her face (and she was never to lose that expression), he hauled down drapes and curtains, overturned furniture, scattered drawers and their frivolous contents across the floor, broke the figurines against the white walls, smashed the mirrors and his reflection there—and then, with a jagged piece of glass, slashed open the silk sofas and chairs so that the down drifted up over the wreckage like small kites. Finally, wielding a heavy curtain rod as if it were a lance, he climbed onto a marble table and swung repeatedly at the large chandelier in the living room, sending the glass pendants winging over the room. With each blow he felt the confusion and despair congested within him fall away, leaving an emptiness which, he knew, would remain with him until he died. He wanted to sleep suddenly, beside his wife, in the room with the Madonna.

A glass spear struck Miranda, who had staggered, weeping and impotent, to the door, and she shrieked. Her outcry was the sound of the trumpet the night before, a high, whinnying note that reached beyond all sound into a kind of silence. The scream broke her paralysis and she rushed at him with a powerful animal grace, the gown flaring open around her bare body, and reaching up caught the rod.

He let it go, but from his high place he leaned down and struck her with his small fist on her head, and the hair cascaded down like a curtain over her stunned face.

He was at the elevator, the automatic door sliding open in front of him, when he heard her frightened, tearful voice calling him down the hall. "Caliban! Caliban! Where are you going? The show! Are you crazy—what about the show tonight? Oh, Mary, full of grace, look what the bastard's done. The place! He's killed me inside. Oh, God, where is he going? Crazy bastard, come back here. What did I do? Was it me, Caliban? Caliban, *meu negrinho*, was it me . . . ?"

APPENDIX:
SELECTED REVIEWS

From *Library Journal*, August 1961

The four short stories which make up this book all have for their leading character an aging man. The first story concerns a retired hospital employee who saved most of his earnings and returned a wealthy man to his native Barbados. Another story is about a college professor who has a brief comeback in teaching after an enforced retirement. The third, laid in British Guiana, traces the career of a dissolute "high-colored" man. The final story about a retiring night club entertainer brings to a climax some of the ideas suggested by the other stories. The theme of age is an unusual one for such a young writer as Mrs. Marshall, but she handles it convincingly. The background color of the exotic locales adds to the book's appeal. Recommended generally.

Adele M. Fasick

Reprinted from Library Journal August 1961. Copyright © 1961 by Reed Publishing, USA, Div. of Reed Holdings, Inc.

From *The New York Herald Tribune*, September 17, 1961

In four short stories keynoted by a title quotation from Yeats, Paule Marshall, the author of "Brown Girl, Brownstones"—published in 1959—has come through with a stellar performance which is something of a renaissance in authentic feeling for real men, women and life. Named for its geographic setting—Barbados, Brooklyn, British Guiana and Brazil—each story describes in terms of natural action how an aging and dying man attempts to face up to the decline of his virile powers. Each man portrayed is conceived in terms of his relationship with a woman; in fact, Mrs. Marshall—herself the mother of a male child to whom this volume is dedicated—is saying that a man is truly a man when he commits himself to a genuine, creative love, and that a woman realizes her womanliness through her man. And she etches character and setting with descriptive power and insight which puts her work up alongside the best of Robert Nathan and her name down as a descendant who has not lost "the flower through natural decension of the soul."

The first story is that of a septuagenarian named Watson who has returned to his native Barbados after fifty years spent in Boston. He is wealthy, but he has not been humanized, and a quiet little servant girl tells him so. The second is about Professor Max Berman, a literary lecher who lures a young colored schoolteacher from Brooklyn to his home in upstate New York. He finds her too much woman for him. The third is about a mixed breed British Guianan whose false pride in ethnic morality locks him out of the life of the woman who could have made something of him. The last is about a distressed clown, his kept partner-woman and the young wife he grasps as he falls. Paule Marshall's art is serious, wholesome and strong.

Henry F. Winslow, Sr.

I.H.T. Corporation. Reprinted by permission.

From *The New Yorker*, September 23, 1961

Four beautifully worked but, unfortunately, quite superficial short novels by a genuinely talented young writer. Each of the stories deals with an elderly man who suffers the final and fatal defeat of his life at the hands of a contemptuous woman. "Barbados," "Brooklyn," "British Guiana," and "Brazil" are the titles and places of the stories, and the four men involved are Mr. Watford, a Barbadian who is struggling to find himself at home after fifty years of hard-working exile in Boston; Max Berman, a cold, sad college professor who schemes pitifully and ruthlessly to warm himself once again at the fires of life; Gerald Motley, a brilliant and once handsome man who wants someone to tell him that his vicious self-mockery has not really destroyed his birthright; and Caliban, an aging nightclub dancer who rebels, childishly, against the sham world that owns him.

Reprinted by permission; © 1961 The New Yorker Magazine, Inc.

From *The New York Times*, October 1, 1961

A few years ago, a young Negro writer named Paule Marshall published "Brown Girl, Brownstones," a fine novel about West Indian Negroes in Brooklyn and the problems of adjustment to a society that was economically and culturally shifting. Now, in "Soul Clap Hands and Sing," she has written four short novels and has extended the theme of Person and Place into the wider range of self-recognition. This extension takes on a very subtle ambivalence because she is again dealing with Negroes. It also points to the fact that the Negro as the subject of a novel is undergoing a considerable change, acquiring new fictional dimensions and associations.

These four short novels are variations on a theme. The men are all middle-aged and "finished," yet they are all desperately trying to grasp at some futile and elusive reassurance. The women are essentially passive instruments who deal the fatal blows which strip away tenuous hopes.

In the first story, a Barbadian farmer who has spent his life in a dry pursuit of advantages is suddenly obsessed by the simple vitality of a girl servant who he has tried sedulously to dehumanize. In the second, a Brooklyn professor, a Jew, becomes sick with desire for a Negro student who symbolizes a primary power he believes would compensate him for all his humiliations.

In the third, a Guianan of mixed blood who has risen to a high professional position becomes convinced that he has been victimized by the false image the world has imposed on him through a woman he loved. In the last, a famous Brazilian comedian is sure that his white partner, whom he has tried to reduce to a puppet, is about to destroy him.

These people are all men and women before they are racially identified. The familiar problem of outer social pressure on the Negro has been subtly and evocatively exchanged for assimilated inner tensions. Miss

Marshall is a penetrating and skillful writer who creates a world as sharp as a scream and with much of the same urgency. Perhaps, in time, more humaneness and compassion will deepen her quite remarkable gifts, and widen her perception. She uses words beautifully, and for this one is profoundly grateful.

Henrietta Buckmaster

From *The Saturday Review*, 1961

"An aged man is but a paltry thing," old Willie Yeats once sang, "A tattered coat upon a stick unless / Soul clap its hands and sing." Paule Marshall, born of Barbadian parents in Brooklyn, has chosen Yeat's bitter, impassioned phrase as the title of her second book, making it the uncommon theme of its four longish stories. The results are both striking and uneven.

Children, we know, have ruled our literary scene, bringing to it the nostalgia of innocence and outrage of experience. They embody the American protest against reality, against time and death. They belong to Hope, bright or betrayed. The aged, however, have remained in a twilight zone, encircled by their loneliness, nodding in the gray shadow of failure. Yet the aged protest against mortality too, and have their literary use. They belong to Memory; they have seen the scarecrow of human illusions laid bare. Hope and Memory still remain the two contending parties in the dreams America dreams.

Though her stories do not all claim America for a setting, Paule Marshall enriches our idea of Memory by gentle, lyrical brooding on the meaning of lives that

have been already spent or shaped. Her four aged protagonists can neither clap nor sing. But they have some
kindlings of rage, and the bitter dignity of knowledge
through defeat. In this lies the unique quality of the
book.

The collection begins well, sags badly in the middle,
and ends with a praiseful burst. "Barbados" is the story
of a Negro hospital attendant who retires, after long
exile in America, to his modest Barbadian plantation.
He is alone, except for the doves he keeps, having fled
all his life the demands of love. The meaning of that
life comes to focus when the warm, unassuming servant girl he harshly ignores rejects him in his moment
of need. "But his inner eye was suddenly clear. For
the first time it gazed mutely upon the waste and pretense which had spanned his years. Flung there against
the door by the girl's small blow, his body slowly crumpled under the weariness he had long denied. He
sensed that dark but unsubstantial figure which
roamed the nights searching for him wind him in its
chill embrace." Setting and action here conspire to cre-
ate a full metaphor of deprivation. "Brooklyn" repeats
the same theme in undistinguished manner.

"British Guiana" attains the length of a novella. It
might have better remained a story. Gerald Motley is
a distinguished drunkard of mixed Chinese, Negro,
and white blood. He dissipates his life in a sinecure
as the director of a radio station. The one true vision
of himself is somehow dispelled by the woman who
loves him most, and who represents "the same and cautious part of himself coming to save him." When many
years after the same woman offers him an important
job, Motley can only howl with ironic laughter. He re-
quests that she grant the opportunity to his protege,
who represents the part of him that refuses to be de-
ceived. Despite its lags, the story has humor and rich

color; its paradoxes cauterize human illusions to heal the flesh of reality.

By far the best story is the last, "Brazil," a sharp yet moving account of a famous comedian about to retire. "O Grande Caliban," as everyone knows him (his true name and his identity seem lost forever), is Rio's implacable jester. A tiny man, he seems all his life a "Lilliputian in a kingdom of giants." "The world had been sealed without him in mind—and his rage and contempt for it and for those who belonged was always just behind his smile, in the vain, superior lift of his head, in his every gesture." Caliban's frenzied effort to reclaim his identity from the posters and cheering crowds, from the stupid, spoiled, blonde Amazon who is his partner, and even from his young, pregnant wife, takes him to the center of his personality and the terrifying slums of Rio. Here all is done with tact and great power.

The example of Caliban shows that an aged man may not be entirely a paltry thing. (Indeed, the sequence of stories in the book reveals a progressive vitality in the characters.) Paule Marshall does not bring new resources of form or startling sensibility to the genre. But she allows her poetic style to be molded in each case by the facts of her fiction: she has escaped the cliches that must doubly tempt every Negro author writing today; and she has given us a vision, precise and compassionate, of solitary lives that yet participate in the rich, shifting backgrounds of culture near and remote. Her retrospective vision is really a forecast of what we may wake up, too late, to see. There is need for a poetics of gerontology.

Ihab Hassan

Reprinted by permission; © 1961 *Saturday Review*, Omni Publications International, Ltd.